BARBARA HANNAY
The Bridesmaid's Best Man

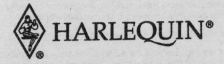

HARLEQUIN®

TORONTO • NEW YORK • LONDON
AMSTERDAM • PARIS • SYDNEY • HAMBURG
STOCKHOLM • ATHENS • TOKYO • MILAN • MADRID
PRAGUE • WARSAW • BUDAPEST • AUCKLAND

ISBN-13: 978-0-373-17490-4
ISBN-10: 0-373-17490-X

THE BRIDESMAID'S BEST MAN

First North American Publication 2008.

www.eHarlequin.com

Printed in U.S.A.

Barbara Hannay was born in Sydney, Australia, educated in Brisbane and has spent most of her adult life living in tropical North Queensland, where she and her husband have raised four children. While she has enjoyed many happy times camping and canoeing in the bush, she also delights in an urban lifestyle—chamber music, contemporary dance, movies and dining out. An English teacher, she has always loved writing, and now, by having her stories published, she is living her most cherished fantasy. This is Barbara's twenty-fifth book! Visit her Web site at www.barbarahannay.com.

CHAPTER ONE

As DUSK settled over the mustering camp, Mark Winchester stepped away from the circle of stockmen crouched around the open fire. He turned his back on them and stood very straight and still, staring across the plains of pale Mitchell grass to the distant red hills.

The men shrugged laconically and let him be. After all, Mark was the boss, the owner of Coolabah Waters, and everyone knew he was a man who kept his troubles to himself.

But as Mark shoved his hands deep in the pockets of his jeans he was grateful the men couldn't guess that his thoughts were centred on a woman. He couldn't quite believe it himself. It didn't seem possible that he was out here, in the middle of the first big muster on this newly acquired cattle property, and still haunted by memories of a girl he'd met in London six weeks ago.

The focus of his life was here—caring for his stock and his land, building an Outback empire. Until now, women had only ever been a pleasant diversion at parties or race meetings, or during occasional trips to the city. But, no matter how hard he'd tried to forget

Sophie Felsham, she had stayed in Mark's head for six long weeks.

Even now, at the end of a hard day's muster, he was staring at the fading sky, at the copper-tinted plains and burnt-ochre hills, but he was seeing Sophie as he'd seen her first in London. He could see her coming down the aisle in a floaty, pale pink bridesmaid's gown, her arms full of pink flowers, her grey eyes sparkling and her lips curved in an impossibly pretty smile. Her skin clear and pale as the moon. So soft.

The crazy thing was, they'd only spent one night together. When they'd parted, they'd agreed that was the end of it. And to Mark's eternal surprise he'd managed to sound as casual about that as Sophie had—as if one night of amazing passion with a beautiful stranger was nothing out of the ordinary.

The next day he'd flown back to Australia. There'd been no fond farewells, no promises to keep in touch. They'd both agreed there wasn't much sense.

Which was exactly how it should have been. It made no sense at all that he'd been tormented and restless ever since.

'Hey, boss!'

Mark swung around, jerked into the present by the excited cry of a young jackaroo, a newly apprenticed stockman.

'There's a long-distance phone call for you,' the boy shouted, waving the satellite phone above his head. 'It's a woman! And she's got an English accent!'

A jolt streaked through Mark like a bullet from an unseen sniper. A stir rippled through the entire camp. The quiet chatter of the men around the fire stopped, and the ringer mending his saddle paused, his long iron needle suspended above the leather. Everyone's amused and curious glances swung to Mark.

He knew exactly what the men were thinking: why would an English woman be ringing the boss way out here?

He was asking himself the same question.

And he was struggling to breathe. He only had to hear the words 'English' and 'woman' in the same sentence and an avalanche of adrenaline flooded his body.

But this phone call couldn't possibly be from Sophie. The only person in England who knew the number of his sat phone was his mate Tim—and Tim knew that only very urgent calls should be made to this remote outpost.

If a woman with an English accent needed to contact him very urgently, she had to be Tim's new bride, Emma. Mark had flown to England to be best man at their wedding, and only last week he'd received an email from the happy couple reporting that they were home from their honeymoon and settling into wedded bliss with great enthusiasm. So what had gone wrong?

Keeping his face impassive, Mark hoped the men couldn't sense the alarm snaking through him as he watched the grinning jackaroo run from the horse truck, waving the phone high like an Olympic torch.

He knew that Emma would only ring him out here if something serious had happened, and his stomach pitched as he was handed the phone.

The boy's eyebrows waggled cheekily, and he muttered out of the side of his mouth, 'She's got a very pretty voice. A bit posh, though.'

A cold glance silenced him and Mark swept an equally stern glare over the knowing smirks on the faces around the fire. Then he turned his back on them again, looked out instead over the holding pens of crowded and dusty cattle, still restless after the day's muster.

An unearthly quiet settled over the camp. The only sounds were the lowing and snorting of the cattle, and the distant trumpets of the brolga cranes dancing out on the plain.

Holding the phone to his ear, Mark heard the line crackle. He swallowed, tasted the acid that always came with the anticipation of bad news, and squared his shoulders. 'Hello? Mark Winchester speaking.'

'Hello?'

The woman on the other end sounded nervous. And the line was bad. Was the blasted battery low?

'Is that Mark Winchester?'

'Yes, it's Mark here.' He fixed his gaze on the red backs of the cattle and lifted his voice. 'Is that you, Emma?'

'No, it's not Emma.'

He frowned.

'It's Sophie, Mark. Sophie Felsham.'

Mark almost dropped the phone.

He swallowed again, which did little to help the sudden tightness in his throat, the flare of excitement leaping in the centre of his chest.

'I don't suppose you expected to hear from me,' she said, still sounding very nervous.

He threw a wary glance over his shoulder, and the men around the campfire quickly averted their eyes, but he knew damned well that their pesky ears were strain-

ing to catch every word. Gossip was scarce on an
Outback mustering camp.

Fighting an urge to leap on a horse and take off for
the distant hills, he strolled away from the camp. Small
stones crunched beneath his riding boots, but the crackling on the line eased. He cleared his throat. Cautiously,
he said, 'This is a nice surprise, Sophie.' And then,
because she'd sounded so nervous, 'Is everything OK?'

'Not exactly.'

A vice-like clamp tightened around Mark's chest as
he kept walking. 'Nothing's happened to Emma and
Tim? They're all right, aren't they?'

'Oh, yes, they're fine. Fabulous, actually. But I'm
afraid I have some rather bad news, Mark. At least, I
don't think you'll like it.'

A fresh burst of alarm stirred his insides. How could
Sophie's bad news involve him?

On the far horizon, the sun was melting behind the
hills in a pool of tangerine. He pictured Sophie on the
other side of the world, her pretty heart-shaped face
framed by a glossy tangle of black curls, her clear, grey
eyes uncharacteristically troubled, her determined little
chin beginning to tremble as her slim, pale fingers
tightly gripped the telephone receiver.

'What is it?' he asked. 'What's happened?'

'I'm going to have a baby.'

He came to an abrupt halt. Went cold all over.

This wasn't real.

'Mark, I'm so sorry.' There were tears in her voice.

He dragged in a desperate breath, tried to stem the
rising cloud of dismay. He couldn't think what to say.

Behind him the cook yelled, 'Dinner's up!' The

ringers began to move about. Chatter resumed. Boots shuffled, and cutlery clinked against enamel plates. Someone laughed a deep belly chuckle.

Around Mark, the red and gold plains of the Outback stretched all the way to the semicircle of the blazing sun fast slipping out of sight. A rogue breeze stirred the grass and rattled the tin roof on the cook's shelter. A flock of white cockatoos flapped heavy wings as they headed for home.

The rest of the world continued on its merry way, while a girl in England began to cry, and Mark felt as if he'd stepped into an alternate reality.

'I—I don't understand,' he said, and then, hurrying further from the camp, he lowered his voice. 'We took precautions.'

'I know.' Sophie sniffed. 'But it—*something* mustn't have worked.'

He closed his eyes.

The very thought that he and the gorgeous English bridesmaid had created a new life sent him into a tailspin. He couldn't take it in, was too stunned to think.

'You're absolutely certain? There's no chance of a mistake?'

'I'm dead certain, Mark. I went to a doctor yesterday.'

He wanted to ask Sophie how he could be sure that this baby was his, but couldn't bring himself to be so blunt when she sounded so very upset.

'How are you?' he asked instead. 'I mean, are—are you keeping well?'

'Fair to middling.'

'Have you had a chance to—' The line began to break up again, the crackling louder than before.

Sophie was saying something, but the words were impossible to make out.

'I'm sorry. I can't hear you.'

Again, another burst of static. He walked further away, fiddled with the setting and caught her in mid-sentence.

'...I was thinking that maybe I should come and see you. To talk.'

'Well...yes.' Mark looked about him again, dazed. Had he heard correctly? Sophie wanted to come here, to the Outback?

He raised his voice. 'I'm stuck out here, mustering for another week. But as soon as I get back to the homestead I'll ring you on a landline. We can make arrangements then.'

There was more static, and he wondered if she'd heard him. And then the line went dead.

Mark cursed. Who the hell had let the damned battery get flat? He felt rotten. Would Sophie think he was deliberately trying to wriggle out of this conversation?

It was almost dark.

A chorus of cicadas began to buzz in the trees down by the creek. The temperature dropped, as it always did with the coming of night in the Outback, but that wasn't why Mark shivered.

A baby.

He was going to be a father.

Again he saw pretty, flirtatious Sophie in her pink dress, remembered the flash of fun in her eyes, the sweet curve of her smile, the whiteness of her skin. The breathtaking eagerness of her kisses.

She was going to be a mother. It was the last thing she wanted, he was sure.

It's the bullet you don't hear that kills you.

He gave a helpless shake of his head, kicked at a stone and sent it spinning across the parched earth. Being haunted by memories of a lovely girl on the other side of the world was one thing, but discovering that he'd made her pregnant felt like a bad joke.

Was she really planning to come out here?

Sophie, the elegant daughter of Sir Kenneth and Lady Eliza Felsham of London, and a rough-riding cattleman from Coolabah Waters, via Wandabilla in Outback Australia were going to be parents? It was crazy. Impossible.

Sophie hugged a glass of warming champagne and hoped no one at her mother's soirée noticed that she wasn't drinking. She couldn't face questions tonight.

She couldn't allow herself to think about her parents' reaction when they learned that their grandchild was on the way. No grandchild of Sir Kenneth and Lady Eliza should have the temerity to be born out of wedlock. And it was so much worse that the baby's father was a man their daughter barely knew, a man who lived with a few thousand cattle at the bottom of the world.

Sophie shuddered as she pictured her parents' faces.

Some time soon they would have to know the worst, but not tonight. It was too soon. She was feeling too fragile.

Fortunately, her father was busy in the far corner, deep in animated conversation with a Viennese conductor. Her mother was equally occupied, relaxed on a sofa, surrounded by a gaggle of young opera hopefuls listening in wide-eyed awe as she recounted highly coloured stories of life backstage at Covent Garden and La Scala.

All around Sophie, corks popped and glasses clinked, and well-bred voices made clever remarks while others laughed. The large room was awash with elegant, brilliant musicians in party mode, and Sophie wished wholeheartedly that she hadn't come.

But her mother had insisted. 'It will be so good for your business, darling. You know you always get a rash of new clients after one of my soirées.'

Sophie couldn't deny that. Besides, this week had been dire enough without getting her mother offside. So she'd come. But already she was regretting her decision.

She was feeling ill and tired, and more than a tad miserable, and Freddie Halverson, a dead bore, was heading her way. Without question, it was time to make a hasty exit.

Slipping out of the room, Sophie hurried up the darkened back stairs to the second floor, and then down the passage to the far end of the house to the little room that had been her bedroom until she was nineteen.

She set the champagne flute on a dresser and flopped onto the window seat, pressed her flushed cheek against the cool pane, and looked out at the faint silhouettes of the rooftops of London, and at the street below that glistened with rain. For the hundredth time, she tried to imagine where Mark Winchester had been when she'd telephoned him this morning.

What was a mustering camp, anyway? Cowboy films had never been her thing.

Twelve long hours had passed since her phone call, but she still felt wiped out and exhausted. Their conversation had been so very unsatisfactory, even though she'd been reassured to hear Mark's voice.

She'd almost forgotten how deep and warm and

rumbly it was. It had reverberated inside her, resounding so deeply she could almost imagine it reaching his baby, curled like a tiny bean in her womb.

But then static had got in the way just when they'd reached the important part, and she'd started to blub! *How pathetic.* After she'd got off the phone, she'd wept solidly for ten minutes, and had washed her face three times.

Now Sophie turned from the window and threw her shoulders back, determined there would be no more crying. She wasn't the first woman in history to find herself in this dilemma.

Problem was, she didn't only feel sorry for herself, she felt sorry for landing this shock on Mark. And she felt sorry for the baby, too. Poor little dot. It hadn't asked to be conceived by a dizzy, reckless girl and a rugged, long-legged stranger with a slow, charming smile. It wouldn't want parents who lived worlds apart, who could never offer it the snug, secure family it deserved.

Just the same, she couldn't contemplate an abortion. She had wanted to explain that to Mark, and would have felt better if she'd been able to—but in the end the phone call hadn't helped at all. She felt worse than before she'd picked up the receiver.

Ever since, she'd been wondering if she'd expected too much of Mark Winchester. After all, they hardly knew each other, and they'd said their goodbyes six weeks ago, had gone their separate ways. She'd tried to forget him, and it had almost worked.

Liar.

Sophie hugged her knees and sighed into the darkness. She could still picture Mark in perfect detail, could see his eyes—dark, rich brown and curiously penetrating. She remembered exactly how tall and broad-shouldered he was, could picture his bronzed skin, the sheen on his dark-brown hair, his slightly crooked nose, the no-nonsense squareness of his jaw.

She remembered the way he'd looked at her when they'd been dancing at the wedding, the quiet hunger that had sent fierce chills chasing through her.

And, of course, she remembered everything that had happened later…the warm touch of his fingers, the heady magic of his lips on her bare skin. She felt a flash of heat flooding her, trembled all over, inside and out— just as she had on that fateful night when they'd been best man and bridesmaid.

There was a soft knock outside. 'Are you in there, Sophie?'

Her best friend's slim silhouette appeared at the doorway.

'Oh, Emma, thank goodness it's you.'

Emma was the only other person she'd told about the baby. Jumping to her feet, Sophie kissed her. 'I didn't expect you to come here tonight. Haven't you and Tim got better things to do?'

'Not when my best friend's in trouble,' Emma said, giving her a hug.

Sophie turned on a lamp, and its glow illuminated the neat orderliness of the room, so different now that it was a guest room. Luckily none of the guests downstairs was using it this evening, and she closed the door.

Cautiously, Emma asked, 'Have you called Mark?'

'Yes.' Sophie let out a sigh. 'But it was pretty disappointing. The line was bad, and we didn't really get to discuss anything important.'

'But how did he take the news?'

'I'm not really sure. He was rather stunned, of course.'

'Of course,' Emma agreed with a small smile. She sat on the edge of the single bed, kicked off her shoes and tucked her legs up, just as she had when they'd been children. 'It would have been a bolt from the blue, poor man.'

'Yes.' Sophie slumped back into the window seat, reliving her dog-awful shock yesterday when the doctor had told her that the tightness in her breasts and the tiredness that had haunted her for the past fortnight had been caused by pregnancy. She'd known she'd missed a period, but she'd been so sure there had to be another explanation, and had been embarrassed beyond belief.

In the twenty-first century, an educated girl was expected to avoid this kind of pitfall. She cringed inwardly, could hear her father's lecture already.

Oh, help.

'Cheer up, Sox.'

Hearing her childhood nickname, Sophie smiled and quickly shoved thoughts of her parents aside. She would deal with them later. *Much* later.

She sighed again, heavily. 'I suppose I was crazy to insist on talking to Mark while he's out in the middle of nowhere, and now I'm going to have to wait another whole week until he gets home and I can speak to him. But I can't think, can't work out what to do about…about *anything* until I've had a chance to talk to him properly.'

'What are you hoping for?'

Unable to give a straight answer, Sophie twisted the locket Emma had given her as a bridesmaid's present.

'That he'll ask you to marry him?' Emma suggested gently.

'Good heavens, no.' She might have been silly enough to get pregnant, but she wasn't so naïve that she believed in fairy tales.

'It's not the easiest option, is it?'

'To marry a man I've known for less than twenty-four hours?' Sophie regarded her friend with a sharply raised eyebrow. 'It wouldn't be very smart, would it?' She gave an annoyed little shrug, and tried to ignore a stab of jealousy. Emma was newly married and blissfully happy with Tim, and *not* pregnant.

'Just the same,' she added quickly. 'I need to know how Mark feels about—well—about *everything*.' Her lower lip trembled as she remembered just how deeply she'd been smitten by him that night. *Stop it*.

'For example,' she said quickly, 'if Mark's going to demand visitation rights there'll be steep air-fares to negotiate.'

Emma slipped from the bed and squeezed onto the window seat, wrapping an arm around Sophie's hunched shoulders. 'It'll work out. You'll feel better once you're able to have a proper talk with Mark, when he gets back from this—' She frowned. 'What did you say he was doing exactly?'

Sophie rolled her eyes. 'Rounding up cattle. But apparently they call it "mustering" in Australia. He seems to be way out in the very centre of the Outback somewhere.'

Emma's upper lip curled with poorly restrained amusement. 'It's hard to imagine Mark Winchester doing the whole cowboy thing in all that heat and dust, isn't it? I mean, he was so wonderfully dashing when he was best man at the wedding. Even I managed to drag my eyes away from Tim long enough to notice how tall, dark and handsome Mark was. And beautifully groomed.'

'Yes,' Sophie agreed with another sigh. 'That was the problem. He was far *too* dashing and handsome. He had such a presence. I wouldn't be in this pickle now if he hadn't been quite so eye-catching.'

'Or if Oliver wasn't such a pig,' Emma added darkly.

Sophie's jaw dropped as she stared at her friend. 'Did you guess?'

'That you started flirting madly with Mark to show Oliver Pembleton that he hadn't hurt you?'

Miserably, Sophie nodded.

'It wasn't hard to figure out, Sox. I know you're not normally a flirt. But I can't blame you for giving it a go at the wedding. Mark was attractive enough to make any girl flutter her eyelashes. And the way Oliver pranced around in front of you with his ghastly new fiancée was insufferable.'

Sophie nodded and felt a momentary sense of comfort that a good friend like Emma understood just how humiliated she'd felt when Oliver had turned up, with his glamorous heiress wearing the sapphire-and-diamond ring originally intended for her.

Practically everyone at the wedding had known she was Oliver's reject. Most had tried not to look sorry for her, but she'd felt their sympathy. It had been smothering. Suffocating. Had sent her a little crazy.

Her good friend let out a huff of annoyance. 'I'm still furious with my mother for letting Oliver come to the wedding. When he broke off with you he should have been axed from the invitation list, but somehow he wangled his way in, plus a fresh invite for *her*, as well.'

'The thing is,' said Sophie, not wanting to dwell on what might have been, 'getting back at Oliver isn't exactly a suitable excuse for getting pregnant. I mean, it's not something I can explain to my parents, is it? Or to my child in the future, for that matter.'

She wasn't sure she could explain to anyone exactly how getting back at Oliver had morphed into getting pregnant with Mark.

But, deep inside, she knew. Her heart could pinpoint the precise moment she'd looked into Mark Winchester's dark eyes and the chatter in her head about Oliver had stopped, and she'd been drawn radically into the present. She'd been suddenly and completely captivated by the magnetic allure of the tall, rangy Australian. It had been like coming out of a deep sleep to find her senses truly awakened for the very first time.

As she'd danced with Mark, her entire body had tensed with an excitement beyond anything she'd ever experienced. Her fingers had longed to touch the suntanned skin on his jaw and, as they'd danced, she'd kept thinking about how his lips would feel on hers.

'So you're definitely going to keep the baby?' asked Emma.

Sophie blinked, then nodded. 'Yes.'

'That's wonderful.'

Was it? Sophie wished she could feel more excited

about the fact that she was going to be a *mother*. It was still so hard to believe.

A heavy sigh escaped her. 'I think I did something silly when I was talking to Mark. I suggested I might come out to see him, so we could talk through what we're going to do about the baby.'

'But that's a fabulous idea. It's exactly what I was hoping you'd do. I told Tim last night—'

'You told Tim about it?'

'Sophie, he's my husband, and he's your friend as well as Mark's best mate. He's worried about both of you. You're so far apart, it's almost like being on another planet. He said last night that if only you two could get together again you'd be able to sort this all out. And I agree.'

'So you think I should go?'

'Absolutely. It's going to be horrendous to try to talk about everything from the opposite ends of the earth.'

That was true. But it would be horrendously extravagant to go all that way for a conversation she could have over the phone.

Except…she would see Mark again. And she might feel stronger about facing her family after she'd spoken to Mark.

And there was always a chance—a tiny, tiny chance admittedly—that when she and Mark got together again, they might…

Be careful, Sophie. Remember what happened with Oliver. Don't get carried away dreaming of a happy-ever-after with Mark.

'Sophie,' insisted Emma. 'It's your future that's at stake. And the baby's and Mark's. This is a big deal. It's not something you can do long-distance.'

'You're probably right,' Sophie said. 'I'll think about it.'

Emma wriggled off the seat, slipped her feet back into her black and silver sandals, then patted the top of Sophie's head. 'Listen to Aunt Emma, darling. If there's a single event when a man and a woman need to sit down and look into each other's eyes while they talk something through, it's a shared pregnancy.'

'I suppose so.'

'I know Marion Bradley's on the lookout for work. She'd take care of your agency for a week or two. Actually, Marion would probably take your business over if she had half a chance.'

'I'll bear her in mind.'

'It'll all work out beautifully.' Emma looked at her watch. 'I promised Tim I'd only be five minutes.'

'You'd better go and rescue him. Thanks so much for coming.'

'I'll be in touch.'

CHAPTER TWO

THE three-quarter moon drifted out from behind a patch of cloud and cast a cool, white glow over the mustering camp. Mark tried to take comfort from his surroundings.

He saw the silvered silhouettes of the sleeping ringers, the last of the tough breed of Outback cowboys who still worked in the saddle, and who were essential help on big musters like this. He stared above at the night sky, at the familiar stars and constellations he'd known all his life. Everything was in the right place, just as it was at this time every year…the saucepan-shaped Orion…the Southern Cross with its two bright pointers…the dusty spill of the Milky Way…

A long sigh escaped him. He'd had twenty-four hours to digest Sophie's news, but he still looked about him with a sense of bewilderment, still felt as if the whole world should have changed to match the sudden turmoil inside him.

He'd made her pregnant.

It was impossible. Astonishing.

He felt so damn guilty.

What the hell was he going to do about it? And what

did Sophie intend to do? He didn't even know if she wanted to keep the baby.

It would be her decision, of course, but he hoped that she would keep it. He would support her, would do the right thing.

He sighed heavily. If only they could have finished their conversation. He blamed himself that the phone's battery had run down. He hadn't realised that the cook he'd hired had a gambling problem. The damn fellow had been using the phone on the sly to place bets with his bookmaker in Melbourne and hadn't bothered to recharge it.

Now, lying in his sleeping swag on the hard, red earth, Mark couldn't stop thinking about Sophie. Kept remembering her gut-punching loveliness. Everything about her had set him on fire—the happy sparkle in her eyes, the musical laughter in her voice, the astonishing smoothness and whiteness of her skin, the seductive tease of her slender body brushing against him as they'd danced.

And then in bed…

He rolled uneasily in his swag. What was the point in tormenting himself with such memories? Sophie wasn't happy now. He'd seduced her and wrecked her life.

When he got back, he would have to bite the bullet and make her understand that there was no point in her coming all the way down here.

Under other circumstances, it would have been different—fantastic, actually—if she'd been coming here. He could think of nothing better than having Sophie arrive for a brief holiday, so that they could take up where they left off. But if she was pregnant? Hell! She might be thinking of something more permanent, and that would be crazy.

His lifestyle was too hard, his world too alien and remote for a pregnant city girl from England. He had a property to run, which meant he was away from the homestead for long stretches. And Sophie would hate it here on her own. Apart from the heat and the dust, everything else was so far away—doctors, hospitals, shops, restaurants. There were no other women handy for girly chats.

It would be much more sensible if they simply worked everything out over the phone. He could send her money and arrange to see the child from time to time.

When he or she was old enough, they would be able to come out here for holidays.

That was the only way to handle this. He would do everything he could to support her, but Sophie shouldn't leave London.

The coffee table in Sophie's lounge was strewn with travel brochures, flight schedules and maps of Australia, as well as flyers advertising her sisters' next concerts.

Sophie stared at an elegant black and white head-shot of her eldest sister, Alicia, and sighed. Both her sisters were musically gifted, like their parents, and both had launched brilliant careers. Neither of them would have landed in a mess like Sophie's.

As the youngest Felsham daughter, Sophie had often been told she was pretty, but she'd been too given to daydreaming and too impulsive to ever be called brilliant. She'd never been able to stick at music practice the way Alicia and Elspeth had, had never felt driven to be a high achiever like her famous parents.

Emma had suggested once that Sophie had stopped

competing with her sisters because she was afraid of failure, and Emma was probably right, but Sophie figured she'd failed often enough to justify her choice.

Oliver's rejection—her most recent and spectacular failure—had been one too many.

Now her unplanned pregnancy would cement her position as the family's very, very black lamb.

Sophie shook her head to clear her mind of that thought. Somehow she had to turn this latest negative into a shining positive. She owed it to her baby.

Of course, she was scared—she'd never had much to do with babies—but she was strangely excited, too. She wanted to be really good at motherhood, was determined to be a perfect mum. Her own mother had always been so terribly busy, especially by the time her third daughter had arrived.

Sophie would be loving and patient, happy to let her baby grow into a little individual, free from the pressures of great expectations.

And for the first time in her life Sophie would be doing something that Alicia and Elspeth hadn't done already and done better than she ever could. She would care for her baby so brilliantly that no one in her family would dare to utter a single 'tut tut'.

Cheered by that thought, she picked up a brochure about the Australian Outback. Her instincts had urged her to go straight to Mark as soon as she'd found out about the baby.

OK, OK, so maybe her instincts had also nudged her clear away from her parents. But, family aside, surely she owed Mark a visit?

Or was she crazy to even think of going all the way

Down Under, to face the possibility of being rejected and hurt yet again?

Closing her eyes, she pictured Mark—remembered his hard, lean body, the tan of his skin, the crinkles at the corners of his eyes, his unhurried smile—and she felt a sudden, thudding catch in her heart. In every way, Mark was very different from Oliver.

Her fingers traced a light circle over her tummy, and she couldn't help smiling. She was carrying a little boy or girl who might look like its daddy, who might walk like him, or smile like him. A whole little person whose future happiness rested in her hands.

And Mark's.

Was Emma right? Did she owe it to her baby to go to Australia, to find Mark in the Outback? But, if she did, what then? What if she fell deeply in love with Mark, only to have him reject her and send her packing? It would be like Oliver all over again only a hundred—no, a thousand—times worse.

Sophie doubted she was brave enough to sacrifice her dignity on that particular altar. But would she be any safer if she stayed here in London to endure the dismayed gaze of her family while she grew fat with this pregnancy?

Wouldn't it be better to take a gamble on Mark?

CHAPTER THREE

THERE was nobody home.

Sophie stared in consternation at the peeling paint and tarnished brass knocker on the front door of the sprawling timber homestead. She read the name plate again: Coolabah Waters. This was definitely Mark Winchester's home.

But no one answered her knock. Where was he?

It had never occurred to her that Mark wouldn't be here. He'd said he would be back before now. Would phone. When she'd called his caretaker to tell him of her plan to fly out here, he had confirmed that Mark was due home any day. But now there was no sign of either of them.

She knocked again, called anxiously, 'Hello!' and 'Anybody home?'

She waited.

There was no answer, no sound from within the big house. All she could hear was the buzz of insects in the grass and the distant call of a lone crow.

She sent a desperate glance behind her, squinting in the harsh Outback sunlight. The mail truck that had brought her from Wandabilla was already a cloud of dust on the distant horizon. Even if she ran after it, jumping and waving madly, the driver wouldn't see her.

She was alone. Alone in the middle of Australia, surrounded by nothing but miles and miles and *miles* of treeless plains and bare, rocky ridges.

Why wasn't Mark here?

She'd thought about him constantly through the long, long flight from England, another flight halfway across Australia to Mount Isa, and then a scary journey in a light aircraft no bigger than a paper plane over endless flat, dry grassland to Wandabilla, near the Northern Territory border. Finally, after getting advice from a helpful woman in the Wandabilla Post Office, she'd cadged a lift to Coolabah Waters on the mail truck.

Now she didn't know what to do. She was exhausted to the point of dropping, and her decision to come all this way to talk to Mark felt like a really, really bad idea—even crazier than inviting him back to her flat on the night of the wedding.

It had been Tim, Emma's husband, who had finally convinced her that she must make the trip Down Under.

'Of course you need to talk to Mark face to face,' he'd insisted. 'He's that kind of guy. A straight shooter. He won't muck you about. And you'll love it in Australia. There's no place like it in the world.'

Well, that was certainly true, Sophie thought dispiritedly, looking about her. But she didn't think she could share Tim's enthusiasm for endless dry and dusty spaces.

She hadn't expected Mark's home to be so very isolated. She'd understood that the Australian Outback would be vast and scantily populated, but she'd thought there'd be some kind of a village nearby at least.

Fighting down the nausea that had been troubling her more frequently over the past fortnight, she tiptoed to a window and tried to peer inside the house. But the glass was covered by an ageing lace curtain, and she could only make out the shape of an armchair.

The window was the sash kind that had to be lifted up. Feeling like a criminal, Sophie tried it, but it wouldn't budge.

Another glance at the road behind her showed that the mail truck had completely disappeared. She was surrounded by absolute stillness, no background noise at all. No comforting hum of traffic, no aircraft, no voices. Nothing.

If she wasn't careful, the silence would rattle her completely.

I mustn't panic.

Sophie sat on her suitcase and tried to think.

Was this her biggest mistake yet?

The family failure strikes again?

Mark could be anywhere on this vast property. She knew there'd been a muster, but she had no idea what other kinds of work cattlemen did. She supposed they kept busy doing *something*. They couldn't simply lounge about the house all day with their feet up, while their cattle ate grass and grew fat.

But, if Mark was off working somewhere on his vast cattle station, where was his caretaker? When she'd spoken to him on the phone, he'd sounded rather nice, with a warm Scottish brogue that had made her feel very welcome.

The abandoned house, however, didn't look particularly welcoming. The veranda was swept, but the floorboards were unpainted and faded to a silvery grey, and the ferns in the big pottery urns were brown-tipped and drooping. The house in general needed a coat of paint, and the garden—well, you couldn't really call it a garden—was a mere strip of straggling vegetation around the house, full of weeds and dried clumps of grass.

Sophie looked at her watch and sighed. It was only ten in the morning, and Mark might be away all day. It was midnight at home. No wonder she felt so exhausted and ill.

Leaving her bags near the front door, she went down the front steps and tottered over the uneven, stubbly grass in her high heels.

Back in London, high heels and a two-piece suit had seemed like a smart idea. She'd wanted to impress Mark. Huh! Now, twenty-six hours and twelve thousand miles later, she felt positively ridiculous. No wonder the fellow in the mail truck had looked amused. She'd probably been his week's entertainment.

She reached the back of the house and found a huge shed with tractors, but no sign of anyone. The house had a back veranda with a partly enclosed laundry at one end. A large glass panel in the back door offered her a view down a long central passage, and an uncurtained window revealed a big, old-fashioned kitchen with an ancient dresser and an enormous scrubbed pine table set squarely in the middle. It was all very neat and tidy, if a bit drab and Spartan.

A large brown teapot on the dresser had a piece of paper propped against it, and Sophie could see that there was a handwritten note on it. A message?

She chewed her lip. She felt wretchedly hot and nauseous. If she didn't get inside soon, she might faint.

She rattled the back-door knob and shoved at it with her hip, but it held firm.

Desperate, she pulled out her mobile phone and stared at it, thinking. The only person she knew in Australia was Mark, but his satellite phone wasn't being answered. If she'd had a phone book, she could have rung the helpful woman in the Post Office in Wandabilla. If only she'd thought to take down her number.

She tried Mark's phone again, with little hope, and of course there was no answer.

She was stuck here, on the outside of this enormous, old shambles of a house, and her stomach warned her that she was going to be ill very soon.

There was only one option, really. She would have to find a way to break in, and she would simply have to explain to Mark later—*if* he turned up.

The louvres beside the back door were promising. She studied them for about five seconds, and then carefully pulled at one. To her utter amazement, it slid out, leaving her a gap to slip her hand through. Straining, with her body pressed hard against the wall, she could just reach the key on the other side of the door. It turned easily, and the door opened.

As Sophie stepped inside, she felt a twinge of guilt and then dismissed it. At least now she could make a cup of tea and find somewhere to lie down. And hope that Mark would understand.

Sundown.

Low rays of the setting sun lit the pink feathery tops

of the grass as Mark's stock horse galloped towards the home paddock, with two blue-heeler cattle dogs loping close behind.

Man, horse and dogs were tired to the bone, glad to be home.

At last.

The past fortnight had been damned frustrating, and quite possibly the worst weeks of Mark's life. He'd been preoccupied and worried the whole time, and desperate to get back early, but then the young jackaroo had thrown a spanner in the works.

A week ago, on a pitch-black, still night before the moon was up, the boy had been standing near the cattle in the holding yard when he'd lit a cigarette. The fool hadn't covered the flare of the match with his hat, and the cleanskins had panicked. In no time their fear had spread through the herd. Six hundred head of cattle had broken away, following the wild bulls back into the scrub, into rough gullies and ravines, the worst country on Coolabah.

It had taken almost a week to retrieve them—time Mark hadn't really been able to spare—but with the bank breathing down his neck for the first repayment on this property he'd needed to get those cattle trucked away.

During the whole exasperating process, he hadn't been able to stop thinking about Sophie and about his promise to ring her. Hadn't been able to hide his frustration, and had been too hard on the men, which was why he'd encouraged the mustering team and plant to travel straight on to Wandabilla now. The men had earned the right to a few nights in town before they headed off to their next job.

Mark had left them at the crossroads because he needed the solitude. Thinking time.

And, now he was almost home, his guts clenched. He had an important phone call to make, possibly the most important phone call of his life.

At last he saw his homestead, crouched low against the red and khaki landscape. It was good to be back. After almost three weeks in the saddle, sleeping in swags on the hard ground, showering beneath a bucket and hose nozzle tied to a tree branch, bathing and washing clothes in rocky creeks, he was looking forward to one thing.

Make that three things—a long, hot soak in a tub, clean clothes and clean sheets. Oh, yeah, and a mattress.

Luxury.

But he attended to his hard working, loyal animals first, washing the dust from them and rubbing his horse down, giving the dogs and the horse water to drink, and food.

He entered the homestead by the back, pulling off his elastic-sided riding boots and leaving them on the top step. He dumped his pack on the laundry floor beside the washing machine, drew off his dusty shirt and tossed it into one of the concrete tubs. Looking down, he saw the dried mud caked around the bottom of his jeans, and decided his clothes were so dirty he'd be better to strip off here and head straight for the bathroom.

He smiled as he anticipated the hot, sudsy bath-water lapping over him, easing his tired muscles. After a good long soak, he'd find his elderly caretaker, irreverently nicknamed Haggis. The two of them would crack open a couple of cold beers and sit on the veranda, while Mark told Haggis about the muster.

After dinner, he would ring Sophie.

His insides jumped again at the thought. He'd gone over what he had to say a thousand times in his head, but no amount of rehearsing had made the task any easier.

The worst of it was, he would have to ring Tim first to get Sophie's number, and he could just imagine Emma's curiosity.

Hell.

Mark reached the bathroom, and frowned. The door was locked.

Splashing sounds came from inside.

Who in the name of fortune…?

'Is that you in there, Haggis?' he called through the door. 'You'd better hurry up, man.'

He heard a startled exclamation and a loud splash, followed by coughing and spluttering. The person inside shouted something, but the words were indistinct. One thing was certain though—the voice was not Haggis's. It was distinctly, unmistakably feminine.

'Who is it?' Mark shouted, his voice extra loud with shock. 'Who's in there?'

Sophie spluttered and gasped as she struggled out of the slippery bath, her shocked heart pounding so wildly she feared it might collapse with fright.

She'd been asleep for most of the day, had woken feeling much better, and hadn't been able to resist the chance to relax in warm water scented with the lavender oil that she'd found in the bottom of the bathroom cupboard. But now her relief that it was Mark Winchester's deep voice booming through the door, and not some stranger's, was short lived. Mark sounded so angry.

She grabbed at a big yellow towel on the rail behind the door. 'It's me, Mark! Sophie Felsham.'

'*Sophie?*'

She could hear the stunned disbelief in his voice.

'When did you get here?' he cried.

Oh, help. He was annoyed. And he sounded impatient.

So many times she'd pictured her first meeting with Mark in Australia, and she'd been wrong on every occasion!

With frantic fingers, she wrapped the towel around her and managed a fumbling knot. 'I'm so sorry, Mark! There was no one home, and I didn't know what to do.'

When there was no response from the other side of the door, she called again, hoping desperately that he would understand. 'I've come out here to see you. So we can talk.'

Then, because it was ridiculous to communicate through a locked door, she opened it.

Oh, gosh.

Bad idea.

Her heart stopped beating.

Mark was...

Totally, totally naked.

Her face burst into flames. 'I—I'm s-sorry,' she stammered. 'I d-didn't realise.'

Mark didn't flinch. There was something almost godlike in the way he stood very still, and with unmistakable dignity, but his silence and his very stillness betrayed his shock. And then a dark stain flooded his cheekbones.

An anguished, apologetic cry burst from Sophie and she slammed the door shut again.

Sagging against it, she covered her hot face with her hands. She hadn't seen a skerrick of warmth in Mark's eyes.

Could she blame him? She wished she could drop

through a hole and arrive back in London on the other side of the globe.

She'd never been so embarrassed.

And yet, as Sophie cringed, a part of her heart marvelled at how fabulous Mark had looked. In those scant, brief seconds, her senses had taken in particulars of his tall, dark, handsome gorgeousness—the hard planes of his chest, the breathtaking breadth of his shoulders, the powerful muscles in his thighs.

Although she'd tried to keep her eyes averted, she hadn't been able to avoid seeing the rest of him—and how very *male* Mark was.

But alien, too, with his dark, stubbled jaw, and suntanned limbs, with the red dust of the Outback clinging to him.

Mark cursed and his heart thundered as he flung open wardrobe doors, grabbed clean clothes and dragged them over his dusty body. It would be some time before he recovered from the sight of Sophie Felsham, in *his* bathroom, wearing nothing but a towel—and the equal shock of standing in front of her like a dumbstruck fool. Stark naked.

Then again, Sophie Felsham wearing *anything* at Coolabah Waters would have stunned Mark.

He swallowed. He'd never dreamed she would arrive here before they'd had a chance to talk.

Why had she come? What did she expect from him?

Leaving his shirt unbuttoned and hanging loose over his jeans, he hurried barefoot down the passage to the kitchen, expecting to find Haggis peeling spuds at the sink, or slicing onions.

He was going to demand answers.

But the kitchen was empty.

It smelled great, however. There was something cooking in the oven—beef and mushrooms, if Mark wasn't mistaken.

And then he saw a piece of paper propped against the teapot. Frowning, he snatched it up.

> *Mark,*
> *My only sister, Deirdre, is seriously ill in Adelaide and I need to visit her. I've tried to call you, but the sat phone doesn't seem to be working. Sorry, mate, but I know you'll understand. I've left frozen meals for you and I've left Deirdre's number beside the phone.*
> *Apologies for the haste,*
> *Angus.*
> *P.S. A young English woman called. She's coming to visit you. Good luck with that one.*

The note was dated four days ago. Mark scratched the back of his neck and wondered when the surprises would stop. He crushed the sheet of paper and tossed it back onto the dresser. He was still trying to come to terms with the twist of fate that had allowed Haggis's trip south to coincide with Sophie's arrival when he heard light footsteps behind him.

'The bathroom's free.'

He swung around, and there was Sophie again. He inhaled sharply.

Her hair was still damp, as if she'd dried it hastily with a towel. Wispy, dark curls clung to her forehead and her soft, pale cheeks. She was dressed in a simple white T-shirt, a slim red skirt, and she wore sandals covered in white daisies.

'Hello again, Mark,' she said shyly.

She hadn't used any make-up, and she looked pale and wide eyed. Incredibly pretty. Impossibly young. Her figure was so slender it didn't seem feasible that it would expand and swell with pregnancy. With his baby.

Something hard and sharp jammed in Mark's throat, and he swallowed fiercely.

'I—I'm really sorry about—' Sophie's mouth twisted into an embarrassed pout, and her eyes widened as she flapped her hands helplessly out to her sides. 'You know—the bathroom and everything.'

'Forget it.' He spoke more gruffly than he meant to, and the back of his neck began to burn.

How should he handle this? Should he greet her formally with a handshake? Ask her if she was feeling well? Throw his arms around her? That would be smart, given the filthy state of him.

Stepping forward quickly, he dropped a quick peck on her soft cheek. She smelled sweet and clean, of shampoo and soap, with a hint of something else. Lavender? 'It's good to see you.'

Super-conscious of his open shirt and unwashed state, he stepped back again. He felt so uncertain. There were so many questions he should ask. *How was your journey? How are you keeping?*

Why have you come?

'I feel terrible about turning up like this,' she said. 'Moving into your home when you weren't even here. I—I thought you said you'd be back last week.'

He nodded slowly. 'I should have been back, but we ran into a spot of trouble.'

'Oh?'

'A big mob of cattle broke away. Took off for the most inaccessible country. Gave us no end of a headache.'

A little huff escaped her, and her shoulders relaxed. 'That sounds like hard work.'

'It was.' He picked up the crumpled note from Haggis. 'I'm sorry my caretaker wasn't here to greet you. He had to go away.'

'Yes, I couldn't help seeing that note.'

It suddenly occurred to Mark that she might have been here for days. 'When did you get here?'

'This morning. I came on the mail truck.'

'The mail truck?' His mouth tilted into an incredulous smile as he tried to imagine Sophie Felsham from London arriving in the dusty township of Wandabilla and asking for directions to Coolabah Waters.

'I hope you don't mind that I used your bathroom. I know there's another one.'

'No. No, of course not.' Mark avoided the unexpected shyness in her eyes. 'You're welcome to it. That's fine.' He ran his fingers through his dusty hair, and remembered that he was still in urgent need of a bath.

Sophie twisted a small, gold locket at her throat. 'I don't make a habit of breaking into people's houses.'

He managed a grin. 'No, you've got the wrong colour hair.' When she looked puzzled, he added, 'You're not Goldilocks.'

Her smile lit up her face, and she looked so incredibly pretty that Mark fought an urge to close his eyes in self-protection.

Sophie pointed to the stove. 'I took the liberty of putting one of your housekeeper's frozen meals in the oven.'

'Good thinking.'

There was an awkward pause while he wondered if he should demand that she explain her presence here. What did she want from him—his support to have an abortion? Money? Marriage?

'Look,' he said, and then he had to stop and take a breath. 'If—if you'll excuse me, I'll make use of the bathroom before I try to be sociable.' He offered her the briefest shadow of a smile. 'I've got half the Outback's dirt and dust on me.'

'Of course,' she said with a dismissive little wave, but her eyes were worried and her cheeks had turned bright pink.

CHAPTER FOUR

She shouldn't have come.

As Mark disappeared back down the passage to the bathroom, Sophie felt completely out of her depth.

In England Mark had been so different—so smooth, and almost passing for a city-dweller in his dark, formal suit—more familiar, less intimidating.

It seemed so silly now, but before she'd left London she'd imagined she would be able to book into a hotel or a motel in a village near Mark's place. She'd planned to call him from there, arrange to meet for a meal in a country tavern, have a nice, long talk. Take it from there…

What an idiot she'd been. She should have quizzed Tim more closely. He could have told her what to expect in the Australian Outback. But the sad truth was, she hadn't really wanted to know too much. She'd been pretty certain a heavy dose of reality would have frightened her off.

Which mightn't have been a bad thing.

But she was here now, so she couldn't back down just yet.

She looked about her, and decided she might as well make herself useful. Perhaps she could set the table for dinner. She crossed the kitchen to the ancient pine dresser to hunt for tablecloths and napkins, then wondered if Mark used the dining room for his evening meal.

It was directly across the passage from the kitchen and, like most of the rooms in this house, had French doors opening onto a timber veranda. This arrangement, Sophie had already discovered, was good for catching breezes and channelling them into the house.

The dining room, like all the other rooms, was a very generous size, but it was also ugly, with tongue-and-groove timber walls painted in a faded, murky green and without a single attractive, decorative touch. In fact, Mark's entire house was as plain and austere as a monk's cell.

It could do with a jolly good makeover—new paint, bright cushions, flowers, pretty fabrics, artwork.

A woman's touch.

Sophie's mind skidded away from that thought. *Not this woman's touch.* She knew for a fact that she couldn't live here.

She opened a door in the sideboard and found a pile of tablecloths—clean but un-ironed, and all of them ancient. Dull and boring. Depressing.

In a drawer, she found red tartan place mats with matching napkins and decided to use them. At least they were colourful. And the silver was clean and shining.

But despite the bright tartan the two place-settings looked rather austere on the huge dining table. She hunted about for a vase or candlesticks, anything to fill in the expanse of bare table-top.

There was nothing.

* * *

Showered and shaved, and neatly dressed in clean clothes, Mark stood in the middle of his bedroom and regarded his reflection in the mirror. He looked ridiculously nervous.

What did Sophie expect from him? Was she hoping for marriage? Surely not.

He'd never considered himself a family man, had more or less decided he was a habitual bachelor. His life was hard, and he worked long hours and took few holidays. He'd never really thought much about marriage, had never found a woman who would make a suitable wife—someone he really admired, who could take the hard life in the Outback.

Now, the irony was that just about any of the Australian girls he'd dated and parted with over the past decade would have fitted the bill better than this woman, with her milk-white English skin and high-flying, London-girl lifestyle.

Except…none of those other girls had been carrying his baby.

Mark glanced again at his reflection, saw concern and confusion, the downward slant of his mouth, and turned abruptly and marched from the room.

When Mark came into the kitchen wearing a crisp white shirt and casual chinos, with his jaw cleanly shaved, he looked so breathtaking that Sophie quickly became very busy, thrusting her hands into oven mitts and heading for the stove.

'This smells wonderful,' she said over her shoulder as she lifted out a pottery casserole dish. 'Your house-keeper must be a good cook.'

'He's a darn sight better than the fellow we had on

the mustering camp.' Mark looked down at the bare kitchen table. 'I'll grab some cutlery.'

'No need. I've set the table in the dining room.'

His eyebrows lifted with momentary surprise.

'Would you rather eat in the kitchen?'

'The dining room's fine.' He gave her a slow smile. 'I wouldn't have expected anything less from the daughter of Sir Kenneth Felsham.'

She gave a flustered little shrug.

'Perhaps I should open a bottle of wine and make it a proper occasion,' Mark suggested as he followed her, carrying the warmed plates through to the other room.

Sophie set the casserole dish down. 'I'm sure wine would be nice, but I'm afraid I can't join you.'

His eyes widened with surprise, and she pointed to her stomach. 'It's not good for the baby.'

'Oh, yes, of course. Sorry. I—I don't really care for wine anyway.'

She looked up quickly to see if Mark was joking, but suddenly it didn't matter if he was speaking the truth or lying through his teeth. Their gazes met and he smiled again, and his smile seemed to reach deep inside her. She had to sit down before her knees gave way.

Goodness. Surely she wasn't going to be all breathless and girly—just as she'd been at the wedding?

Mark sat, too, and indicated that she should help herself to the food. Her hand trembled ever so slightly as she lifted the serving spoon, and she was sure he noticed.

'You must be feeling rather jet-lagged,' he suggested.

She nodded, glad to hide behind this excuse, spooned beef and mushrooms onto her plate, and hoped Mark was the kind of man who liked to fill his stomach before he tackled difficult discussions. But when she looked up she found his dark eyes regarding her thoughtfully.

She pointed to the food. 'I'm sure you must be ravenous. Don't let this lovely dinner get cold.'

Without comment, he helped himself to the food and began to eat with some enthusiasm, but it wasn't long before he put his fork down. His throat worked, and he lifted his napkin from his lap and set it on the table.

'I can't help wondering why you've come all the way out here,' he said. 'I told you I'd telephone as soon as I got back.'

'I know, Mark.' Sophie felt as if a piece of meat had stuck in her throat. She swallowed. There was nothing there, but the feeling wouldn't go away. 'I—I thought it would be easier for us to talk face to face. I didn't like the idea of trying to discuss matters like child support and visiting rights over the phone. It—it seemed rather tacky.'

Her heart thumped madly, and she felt completely intimidated by his frowning silence.

At last he said, 'So you're planning to have the baby?'

Oh, heavens. Was he going to ask her to have an abortion?

She drew herself very straight. 'Yes. Absolutely.'

She fancied she saw a flash of relief in his eyes, but he didn't smile.

Under the table, she crossed her fingers. *So far, so good.*

Mark's gaze narrowed. 'And you're quite certain I'm the father?'

Sophie gasped. 'Of course. How can you ask that?'

He shrugged. 'I had to make certain. For all I know, you might do this kind of thing all the time.'

'What kind of thing?'

'Come on, Sophie. You know what I'm talking about.'

'No.'

His jaw tightened, and for the first time he looked uncomfortable. 'One-night stands. Casual sex with strangers.'

She flinched as if he'd physically hit her.

Casual sex with strangers.

She knew that was what their wonderful night had amounted to, but somehow she'd hoped that Mark might have looked on it with finer sentiments. Her baby's conception hadn't been sordid. But perhaps she'd romanticised it out of all proportion.

Mark must have seen the shock in her face. His expression softened immediately. 'I just think we should lay our cards on the table,' he said more gently.

'The baby's yours, Mark.' She lifted her chin high. 'I don't make a habit of casual flings. There's been no one else. Do you really think I would come all this way and single you out if it wasn't your child? Why would I bother?'

He nodded slowly. And then, as if he needed to hide his feelings, he looked down at the table cloth and cleared his throat. 'I'm prepared to help with any money you need.'

'Thanks. I might need to…to find a bigger flat. I'm not sure if I'll manage paying everything for the baby as well.'

'I wouldn't expect you to.' His long brown fingers folded a corner of the tartan table mat down then smoothed it out again, and a muscle in his jaw tightened into a hard little knot. 'I'm assuming you plan to have the baby in England? To be a single mother—at least for the time being?'

A hot, stinging sensation troubled Sophie's eyes. Oh,

damn, she wasn't going to cry, was she? Mark's assumption was perfectly logical. Sensible.

She'd never really believed that she could come to Australia, get to know Mark better and start a relationship with him. But she hadn't been able to squash a tiny hope. Now she felt very foolish.

Mark cleared his throat. 'I assume you're not here to discuss marriage.'

'No! Of course not!' she cried with unnecessary passion, almost tearfully. She blinked away the wretched dampness. What was the matter with her? 'I'm certainly not expecting you to marry me. We hardly know each other.'

The tiniest hint of a smile glowed in Mark's dark eyes, and Sophie knew he was thinking about their night together. Her heart seemed to bounce inside her.

He dropped his gaze to the table. 'I guess the thing that still puzzles me is why you've come all this way,' he said quietly. 'All you said you want from me is child support, but you could have asked for that over the phone.'

He looked up quickly and his dark eyes probed her. 'So what's the deal, Sophie? Where do you want to take things from here?'

It was a very good question.

But, when Mark frowned at her like that, Sophie felt so suddenly flustered and confused she couldn't remember the answer.

Her mouth went very dry. 'I suppose...' She swallowed. 'I suppose I wanted to be sure.'

His response was a look of intense bewilderment. "What about?"

Oh, help. Couldn't Mark guess how hard it was to explain the confusing, scary, almost intangible *something* that had pushed her here almost against her will? 'I—I think I wanted to be sure about—' Again she swallowed, and moistened her lips with her tongue. 'About us.'

She didn't look at him now, simply rushed on to explain. 'I've been feeling so confused. Everything happened so quickly. You've no idea how crazy it was to find myself pregnant after just one night.'

Her mouth trembled dangerously and she shoved a hand against her lips.

'And it was my fault entirely,' Mark said.

Not entirely, she thought, remembering how madly she'd flirted.

His face twisted into a complicated, fiercely gentle smile. 'At the very least, I should have stayed for one more night.'

Sophie wanted to smile back at him, but instead she spluttered tearfully, 'See? That's my point. I didn't even know you had a sense of humour.'

And then she burst into noisy tears.

She heard the scrape of Mark's chair on the timber floor, and next moment his deep voice was rumbling sexily beside her. 'Come here,' he said, taking her arms and pulling her gently out of her chair.

Holding her against his chest, he wrapped his arms around her, and she had no choice but to cling to him while her tears had their way.

'Hush,' he whispered, brushing a path of soft kisses over her brow and onto her cheeks.

'I'm so sorry, Mark.'

'Don't be,' he murmured, running a slow hand down her shaking spine.

'I don't want to cry like this.'

'Cry as much as you like. From where I'm standing, it feels great.'

That brought her to her senses. She pulled away, and immediately felt an awful sense of loss. Using the backs of her hands, she cleared tears from her eyes.

Mark was looking at her with a mixture of tenderness and concern that did all sorts of wicked things to her insides.

'There ought to be an instruction manual for this sort of thing,' he said as he shoved his hands into his trousers. 'But you will stay here for a while at least, won't you?'

Goodness! Was this the opening she'd hoped for?

Sophie wanted to hug him, but instead she said carefully, 'It would give us a chance to get to know each other better.'

And then, in case he changed his mind, she hurried to add, 'I can't stay here for very long. There's someone minding my business, and I have to see doctors, have antenatal checks and scans. That sort of thing.'

Mark smiled kindly. 'But, if you stayed for a couple of weeks, it would be an improvement on one night.'

She nodded. 'Indeed.'

'I guess we owe it to the baby, don't we?'

'Well, yes. I suppose it *would* be rather embarrassing to admit to our child that I know nothing about its father, apart from his name and the colour of his eyes.'

Mark's dark-brown eyes held hers. They shimmered with subtle innuendo, flooding Sophie with memories of their night together, sending a high-voltage flash scorching through her.

'You know a lot more about me than that,' he said.

Instinctively, in self-protection, she lowered her lashes. Her wanton behaviour on that night still bewildered her. To have been so suddenly carried away was completely out of character.

What if she fell deeply in love with Mark now, but he didn't love her back? She couldn't bear a repeat of what had happened with Oliver. Somehow, she knew that a break up after falling in love with Mark would be much, much worse.

'I'll stay for two weeks,' she said carefully. 'We should be able to sort out your paternity arrangements by then.'

Mark grinned, and his hands came out of his pockets as he reached for her again. She knew that he wanted her in his arms, wanted to kiss her.

But wasn't that crazy?

'What's the matter?' asked Mark.

'I—I—um—*don't* think we should get too intimate, do you?'

'Why ever not?' He smiled gorgeously as he reached for her. 'Isn't the harm done? We'd be shutting the stable door after the horse has bolted.'

Heavens! She had to be careful, had to remember that staying here was risky. She had no idea if she and Mark could make a relationship work. And she had no idea how she could possibly be happy in the drab, monotonous Outback.

There were no shops around the corner. No little village nearby. No friendly faces. Nothing and no one for fifty miles at least.

Mark's big hands circled her waist, but Sophie planted her hands firmly over his to prevent his from moving. If she was to get through the next two weeks with her heart intact, she had to be clear headed and strong minded. Disciplined.

'We need to get to know each other as friends, not as lovers,' she said.

'Why not both?'

Mark looked deeply into her eyes, and her breath shivered in her throat. His hands were warm and strong beneath hers. Her blood fizzed in her veins.

His serious brown gaze studied her, as if he was trying to read how she really felt about this. 'You really mean it? You just want to be friends?'

No, she wanted to cry, but she forced herself to be sensible. 'I'll be leaving in two weeks' time, Mark. And—and I don't think we should make our situation any more complicated than it already is.'

'Friendship,' Mark murmured softly, but then, before Sophie knew quite what was happening, his hands were cupping her face and she was beginning to melt.

She tried to protest, but there was something too impossibly mesmerising about Mark Winchester when he was moving in for a kiss.

And yet incredibly, at the last moment, when his lips were a mere millimetre from hers, she managed a pathetic objection. 'Mark, we mustn't!'

'Shh,' he murmured against her mouth.

Valiantly, she ignored the delicious tremors dancing all over her skin and she tried again. 'But we've settled for friendship, right?'

'Whatever you say,' he replied lazily, and then he kissed her.

His lips were soft and warm, and his skin smelled clean and faintly of aftershave. His kiss was slow and dreamy, and Sophie's resistance melted like butter in summer. She leaned into him and gave herself up to the unhurried pressure of his lips, the sexy caress of his tongue, the rough, manly texture of his jaw against hers.

Ages later, when he pulled away and smiled into her eyes, every part of her was zinging and zapping with happiness, but she tried to tell him off.

'You weren't supposed to do that,' she said breathlessly.

'Neither were you.'

Well, yes, that was true. She'd kissed Mark with regrettable enthusiasm.

She wished she could think of a cutting remark to wipe the knowing smile from his face, but his kiss had made her woozy and warm and slow witted. Cutting remarks had never been her strong point anyway.

Just the same, as common sense returned she became very busy, gathering up their plates and marching to the kitchen to stack the dishwasher. And, using jet lag as her excuse, she went to bed early without any more kisses.

Mark stood at his bedroom window, staring out into the black, still night.

Friendship.

That was a rum deal.

All he could see was Sophie's lips, pink and trembling. He'd been desperate to taste her, and her kiss had sent him spinning. When her lovely body had melted against him, he could have sworn that her response was as eager as it had been in London.

But she wanted friendship.

At least, she'd *said* she wanted friendship. Her body had said something else.

He cursed softly.

What was a man to do? How was he supposed to live here alone, with a woman as alluring as Sophie, without wanting to hold her?

What a crazy situation.

He and Sophie should have been able to say goodbye in England and continue on their merry, separate ways. She could have done whatever it was that she did in London and marry some Brit—someone like Tim, or one of those other fellows he'd met at the wedding. Mark could have continued getting his property in order.

Instead, Sophie was going to be here on his turf, under his roof, for two weeks. For fourteen days and nights he would be seeing her, smelling her, wanting to make love to the most delectable, desirable woman he'd ever met.

Mark watched an owl fly across the path of the moon, and let out a heavy sigh. Sophie was probably wise to be wary of more complications. She'd already had more than her share of problems after their one night in London, and when her two weeks were up she should be free to fly home without the burden of extra emotional baggage.

It might have been different if they'd been considering an ongoing relationship, but they both knew there wasn't much point. He could never get a decent job in London, and she was totally unsuited to life at Coolabah Waters.

Damn it. She was right. Friendship was their best option.

He let out a low curse. Why did making the right choice have to feel so wrong?

Sophie lay in bed, staring above her at the fan dangling from the ceiling. After the heat during the day, the night was surprisingly cool, so she hadn't turned it on. She'd left the curtains open so that silvery moonlight could stream through the window. In this light, the paintwork didn't look quite so bad.

But she couldn't sleep.

She was thinking about Mark's kiss and how easily she'd given in. And as she lay there in the moon-washed dark, she was remembering the night they'd met. She'd put up such little resistance that night it had been shameful.

Ever since, she'd been trying not to think too much about it, but perhaps it was important to remember. If she was going to be with Mark for a whole fortnight, that night should serve as a warning….

CHAPTER FIVE

'COME outside with me.'

That was how it had started—with words that had been ringing alarm bells for women since time began.

The wedding reception was almost over, and Emma and Tim had already left for their honeymoon.

'Everyone else will be leaving soon, so come on,' Mark urged. 'Let's take a walk in the garden.'

Sophie knew it was a line and, after the way she'd shamelessly flirted with Mark all evening, she couldn't really blame him for trying. But she was quite sure she would decline his invitation.

'I should help Emma's mother to pack up her wedding dress.'

Mark took Sophie's hand and sent a rush of thrills up her arm. 'There's a swarm of aunts to help her. She doesn't need you. Come on. It's a very important tradition—the best man and the bridesmaid—'

'Dance briefly, as part of the wedding waltz,' Sophie said very firmly as she tried to ignore the effect of his hand on her.

Mark's dark eyes gleamed, and he smiled at her. 'But then they briefly go outside together.'

Sophie laughed and rolled her eyes. 'Do you have much success using that kind of line with Australian girls?'

'Works like a dream every time.'

'I don't believe you. I've met Aussie girls. They're usually very savvy about men.'

'And how many Australian men have you met?'

She had to admit, 'Very few.'

He took her hand. 'Where I live in the Outback, we have almost all our parties outdoors. Under the stars.'

'What are you telling me, Mark? That you're feeling cooped up from being inside a building for too long?'

He grinned. Gorgeously. And Sophie knew she'd played right into his hands. But, strangely, she didn't mind. She'd been feeling miserable for weeks, and tonight, for the first time in ages, she was having a really good time.

In fact, 'good time' was something of an understatement. When she'd danced with Mark she'd been so entranced, so captivated and turned on she'd almost melted on the dance floor.

The look on Oliver's face had been very satisfying.

OK…so there was an undertone of gratitude in her smile as she stepped out into the June evening with Mark. But she felt inexplicably happy, too. The simple act of walking beside the Thames and holding hands had never been more exciting.

Sophie couldn't help but be flattered by all the curious glances they attracted. Mark looked unbelievably handsome in his dark formal evening-suit, and she felt like a film star in her dreamy bridesmaid's gown.

To Mark's disappointment, they couldn't see many stars. London was too brightly lit and the buildings were too tall. But they talked happily.

He told Sophie how he'd met Tim when Tim had gone to Australia in search of an Outback adventure during his gap year.

'Tim ended up working as a jackaroo on my family's property near Rockhampton,' Mark said. 'We became great mates, and we've been friends ever since.'

'That's rather unusual, considering how far apart you live,' Sophie remarked. 'There must have been a lot of phone calls and emails.'

He nodded. 'But we've travelled, too. We've met up at cricket test matches, and a couple of rugby grand finals.'

Sophie told him how she'd known Emma since kindergarten.

'And I organised the musicians for the wedding,' she said. 'I'm an agent for musicians. I hire bands, singers, string quartets, that sort of thing.'

'One of the wedding guests was telling me about all the musicians in your family. Oliver Pebble—no—Pemble-something…'

'Oliver Pembleton,' Sophie mumbled, not at all happy to have that name thrown into the conversation.

'That's it. He seemed to think it was his duty to fill me in about your famous connections.'

'Oh, yes,' she sighed. 'He *would.*'

'If I remember correctly, your father's an orchestral conductor, your mother's an opera singer and your sisters perform as soloists all over Europe?'

Sophie nodded.

'Very impressive. But I'm ashamed to confess I've never heard of any of them till tonight.'

'Bless you!' Sophie let out a hoot of laughter and clapped her hands. Linking her arm through Mark's, she gave it a squeeze. 'I usually have to spend hours listening to people rave on about my family. It gets very tedious explaining that I really don't have any musical talent and that's why I'm an agent and not a performer.'

'So what's your talent?' Mark asked her.

She held up her hands. 'Double-jointed thumbs.'

But then she felt silly and childish, even though Mark was kind enough to laugh.

'What else?' he prompted her.

'I make amazing desserts,' she offered, keen to atone for her gaffe.

'Really? Now, that's an impressive talent. My house-keeper doesn't know any fancy desserts. All I get is the plain stuff. Tinned fruit and ice cream.'

He looked down at her with a wistful, little-boy smile.

'Poor you,' she crooned, and then, unbelievably, she made a fateful mistake. 'I have three-quarters of a lemon-chiffon pie in my fridge.'

Mark grinned. 'And where's your fridge?'

'Don't be greedy. You've already eaten dessert tonight.'

'I know, but where's your fridge?'

She told him.

And before she knew what was happening he'd hailed a taxi.

OK, on the surface it *did* look as if she was very foolish and naïve. She'd normally never dream of taking a man she'd just met back to her flat. But, honestly, she did know she was leaping into dangerous waters. Mark was gorgeous and he'd been such good company, and she couldn't remember an evening when she'd felt so comfortable with a man she'd just met.

When they got back to her flat, she gave Mark a huge helping of lemon-chiffon pie and whipped cream, and a tiny helping for herself to be companionable.

'This is amazing,' he said, his face lit by a smile that seemed very close to rapture. 'It's by far the best dessert I've ever eaten.'

Sophie grinned. 'I told you I was talented.'

She put their bowls and spoons in the sink, and when she turned she found Mark standing close behind her.

That was when she made the *biggest* mistake of the night.

Perhaps she could blame Oliver for being a rat, or she could blame Emma for getting married. Sophie and Emma had been planning their weddings since they'd been nine years old, and she was feeling sentimental, wanted a little romance for herself.

Or maybe Mark was simply and utterly irresistible. Whatever…

'What's your talent, Mark?' she asked him breathlessly.

'I'll show you,' he murmured.

Later, she would cringe at the corniness of it. But at the time she didn't mind a jot, because Mark was already kissing her. His mouth was warm and deliciously seductive. And when he slipped his arms around her their bodies meshed perfectly, and sparks erupted in so many parts of Sophie that she desperately needed to discover every one of Mark's talents.

Her world had fallen apart as easily as that.

Now, as she lay in the back bedroom at Coolabah Waters, her hand pressed to her still-flat stomach,

Sophie was miserably aware of the fallout from that one careless, blissfully romantic night.

To add to her mood of general gloom, the moon disappeared behind a bank of clouds, leaving her bedroom swathed in darkness. The fading paintwork, the ceiling fan and the cane chair in the corner disappeared into the suffocating black of the Outback night. She couldn't see a thing, and she couldn't remember where the light switch was. She felt panic stir.

From deep within the house there came a creaking sound, and hairs rose at the back of Sophie's neck. *What was that?*

A footstep?

It couldn't be Mark coming to her room, could it? He wouldn't do that, would he?

Alone in the dark, she was pitifully aware of how little she knew about the father of her baby. He'd seemed gentlemanly enough in London—when he hadn't been busily seducing her. This evening, although he'd kissed her, he'd kept his distance when she'd asked him to. But could she be sure she could trust him?

She heard another sound, another creak, and her ears strained for the soft fall of footsteps. Could he be moving about barefoot?

Her heart began to pound. If only it wasn't so dark. If only she wasn't here all alone with him in the middle of the big, empty Outback! If only she wasn't such a trusting fool!

Good grief, she'd acted on some crazy impulses in her time, but surely coming here to Outback Australia was the worst, the craziest thing she'd ever done. She was alone out here with one man. A man she barely knew. A man who would much rather have sex with her than stay alone in his room down the hallway.

Again, she heard a creak.

Logic told her that it could be the iron roof, or the old house's timbers shifting in the cooling air. But in the pitch-black, all alone in a strange bed, Sophie's fear won out over logic.

Her heart thumped wildly and she leapt out of bed. Hands groping in front of her, she felt her way across the room to the door and kicked her foot on a chest of drawers, before she found the solid, old-fashioned key in the lock and turned it.

Mark slept badly, and as luck had it the phone rang shortly after dawn. He snatched it up quickly, afraid that its ringing would reach Sophie's room and disturb her.

Sinking groggily back onto his pillows, he mumbled, 'Good morning.' He blinked when he realised the caller was Tim.

'Apologies for calling so early, Mark, but Emma badgered me. Claims she can't rest till she knows if Sophie has reached your place in one piece.'

'Oh, sure,' Mark said, hefting onto one elbow and squinting at his bedside clock—it had just gone five. 'Sophie got here yesterday. She's fine.'

'Thank God for that.'

Mark heard Tim relaying the news to his wife, and then Emma's voice issuing some kind of instruction. 'I'm not going to tell him that,' Tim hissed in a poorly disguised stage whisper. 'Of course he'll be nice to her.'

Mark sank back onto the pillow and rolled his eyes

at the ceiling. 'Tell Emma I'll handle Sophie with kid gloves,' he said. 'I'm a very nice guy.' *Despite having made the poor girl pregnant.*

'I told Em she was worked up about nothing,' Tim said. 'But she's worried because of what happened last time.'

'Last time?' Mark frowned and scratched the back of his neck. 'What are you talking about? What last time? Surely Sophie hasn't been pregnant before?'

'No, mate. Nothing like that. But hasn't she told you about her ex?'

An uneasy pang circled Mark's heart. 'No. What about him?'

'Downright cad of a boyfriend. Dropped her cold a few months ago, just as they were about to announce their engagement.'

The pang in Mark's heart arrowed through his guts. 'Really?'

'Sophie was hurt rather badly,' Tim said. 'Understandable, of course, but she's a tender-hearted little thing. Was absolutely gutted when he turned up with a new fiancée just a few weeks later.'

Mark drew a sharp breath.

'That's why Emma and I are thrilled that the two of you have hit it off,' Tim added. 'Bad luck about the unplanned pregnancy, of course, but I'm sure you'll work something out.'

Mark swallowed, couldn't bring himself to reply.

'At least we know we can rely on you to play it straight with Sophie,' Tim said.

'Yes,' Mark said faintly. 'Of course.'

When Tim said goodbye, Mark stared grimly at the

receiver. Throwing his bed clothes aside, he launched himself out of bed and paced his room, aware of the anxious ache that had settled in the pit of his stomach.

Bloody hell. Poor Sophie. Dumped by one man, made pregnant by the next. Talk about leaping out of the frying pan into the furnace.

He sighed heavily, ploughed frantic fingers through his hair. He'd assured Tim that he would 'play it straight' with Sophie. And that was right. He had no intention of stringing her along with false promises. But was that enough?

Last night they'd both agreed that marriage wasn't really an option, but was Sophie secretly hoping for a proposal from him? Or was she extra wary of commitment, after her experience with this other jerk?

Last night she'd been nervous when he'd tried to kiss her. But then she'd liked it.

No doubt the poor girl was as confused as he was.

It was beginning to make sense now.

It made no sense at all.

Sophie slept in.

When she still hadn't emerged from her room at half-past ten, Mark made a pot of tea and toast with marmalade, piled everything onto a tray and knocked on her bedroom door.

There was no answer, and he told himself that it was to be expected. The woman was tired and jet-lagged.

Just the same, an unreasonable fear sent alarm creeping through him like spiders.

He set the tray on the floor and tried to open the door, and was surprised to discover that it was locked.

He knocked again carefully, and then called, 'Sophie? Are you all right?'

Still no sound.

He felt something close to panic, considered his options and was about to force the door with his shoulder when he heard a muffled sound.

A voice called faintly. Then silence again. His heart hammered as he imagined all sorts of dreadful possibilities. 'Sophie!' he cried. 'What's the matter?'

At last he heard footsteps on the bare-timber floor, the rattle of the key, and finally the door squeaking open on rusty hinges.

Sophie stood before him in a fine, white cotton nightgown rendered transparent by the morning sunlight pouring through the window behind her. Mark's breathing faltered. She was so exquisite—her lush curves and slenderness balanced in perfect proportion. He was grateful he'd already set the tray down or he might have dropped the lot.

Sweeping a tumble of dark curls out of her eyes, she smiled shyly.

'Good afternoon, Sleeping Beauty.' He was dismayed that his voice sound ragged and off-key, as if he'd run out of breath.

'What time is it?' she asked, blinking sleepily. 'Have I slept in?'

With commendable restraint, Mark kept his gaze strictly on her face. 'It's just gone half-past ten. I wasn't sure how long I should leave you.'

'Heavens, I'm glad you woke me.'

He retrieved the tray and Sophie's eyes widened.

'You've made breakfast, Mark? How kind.' But

then she sagged against the door frame, groaned weakly, pressed a hand to her stomach and another against her mouth.

'What's the matter?' Mark cried, feeling helpless as he stood there with the tray.

She whispered, 'I need to use the bathroom.' Moaning softly, she pushed at him with a frantic hand.

He sprang back, giving her a clear path as she stumbled wretchedly down the hallway.

Hell. Last night he'd been fantasising about seducing this woman.

This was reality, he thought as he heard distressing sounds coming from the bathroom. This was Sophie Felsham's life for the next seven months—morning sickness, a baby growing inside her, stretching her body beyond recognition, and finally the frightening pain of giving birth. The responsibility of a new life, and the round-the-clock care of a baby.

And what was Mark's role—to watch from the side-lines?

What a damned crazy situation! Sophie had been trying to recover from one disastrous relationship when she'd been landed with this. And Mark was totally implicated, utterly guilty, but unsure exactly what she wanted from him.

Suddenly, two weeks didn't seem nearly long enough for them to work out a solution.

Sophie felt much better when the dash to the bathroom was over and she'd washed her face, cleaned her teeth and combed her hair.

She came back into the bedroom and was surprised

to find that Mark was still there, his eyes sympathetic. Worried.

'Does that happen every morning?'

'Just about.'

He shook his head, gave her a rueful smile. 'It's not fair, is it?'

'Oh, it could be worse. At least it's only first thing in the morning. Some poor women are sick all day long.' She sat on the edge of the bed and looked at the tray laden with tea and toast.

'I wasn't sure if you'd still want breakfast,' he said. 'But if you like, I'll make a fresh lot.'

'Don't bother. This will be fine, thanks.'

'It'll be cold.' He reached to take the tray. 'Let me make you some more. You hop back into bed. Put your feet up. This won't take a minute.'

'You're spoiling me,' Sophie protested, but she did exactly as she was told.

She remembered her middle-of-the-night fears about Mark, and felt a twinge of guilt. He couldn't have been nicer or more caring if he'd been a loving husband.

It was irrational of her, but she found his kindness disconcerting. She couldn't shake off her fear that she might fall in love with him and get hurt. What if she got to the end of these two weeks and found that she wanted to stay with him, while Mark was more than happy to let her go?

Where's your stiff upper lip, Sophie? No need to throw in the towel just yet.

'Fresh tea and hot toast,' Mark said a little later, returning as promised in a jiffy, and setting the tray carefully on her bedside table.

'Mark, you're an angel. A knight in shining denim.'

He looked embarrassed and put his thumbs through the belt loops in his jeans. 'I'll leave you to have it in peace. Take as long as you like.'

Sophie enjoyed her breakfast immensely. She couldn't remember ever having eaten breakfast in bed before, not unless she'd made it for herself, and that didn't count. Afterwards, she dressed and took her tray to the kitchen, where she found Mark at the sink washing dishes.

For a moment she paused, rather stunned by the sight of this tall, mega-masculine cattleman dressed in battered jeans and a long-sleeved blue cotton shirt, engaged in such a domestic task. Her mind conjured a disturbing image of his strong, workmanlike hands tending to a little baby—bathing her, changing her nappy, laughing and blowing kisses while he chattered in baby talk.

Good grief. If she didn't get a grip on her imagination, she was going to find herself in no end of trouble.

Luckily the phone rang, providing a distraction. Mark wiped his hands on a towel and grabbed the receiver from the wall. He frowned as he concentrated on the caller's message. 'OK. I'll come straight over,' was all he said, and then he hung up.

Sophie couldn't help wondering what this meant. Where was Mark going? Would she be involved?

His face was grim as he looked at her. 'That was my neighbour, Andrew Jackson. There's been an accident. A truck full of cattle has rolled coming out of a creek crossing.'

'That sounds bad. Is anyone hurt?'

'I don't think so. But it's on my boundary, so I'll have to head over there and see what I can do.'

'Oh.'

Sophie gulped.

At home there would be police, ambulances and the fire brigade all rushing to the scene of an accident. But the Outback was so remote that people had to depend on their neighbours to help them out. How scary was that?

'How will you be able to help, Mark?'

'Hard to say. I might be able to give them a hand to jack up the truck. Or I might have to use the winch on the four-wheel drive to pull them upright.' He shrugged. 'They might need assistance with injured cattle.'

'I—I see.' Sophie felt more than a little out of her depth. 'I don't suppose I'll be any use?'

He smiled. 'You'd be much better off resting here.'

That puts me in my place—the useless English girl.

Sophie hated the thought of being left alone again. Was this the fate of all Outback women? To be abandoned while their men ran around being heroes?

'What can I do, Mark?'

About to rush off, he paused, framed by the flyscreen door, then he came back into the room and touched her lightly on the elbow. 'You'll be OK here, won't you?'

No, she wouldn't be OK. She'd been looking forward to spending a whole day with Mark, but she couldn't bear him to think of her as a wimp. 'I'll be fine,' she assured him, holding her head high.

If this was the sort of thing that happened on Mark's property, then she was determined to try and fit in. No matter how scared she was, she had to make the best of it. 'Can I fix you a snack to take with you?'

Mark's eyes warmed in a way that made Sophie's blood sing. 'Some tea would be terrific. Can you put it in a flask? I'm going to load a few things into the ute.'

'All right.'

Sophie was glad she'd snooped in Mark's kitchen yesterday so she knew where things were. She flew to the kettle, and while the water was coming to the boil she collected bread, butter, cheese and pickles and began to make sandwiches. By the time Mark returned, the tea was in a flask, the sandwiches wrapped and in a paper bag along with oatmeal biscuits and an orange.

'This should keep you going,' she said, handing them to him.

He looked both surprised and delighted. 'Thanks.' With his free hand he drew her close, pressed a kiss to her forehead. It was only the lightest brush of his lips, but it sent a thrill from her breastbone to her toes.

A small gleam came into his eyes as he let her go and then he turned abruptly, snagged a wide-brimmed hat from a rack on the wall and set it on his head at a careless angle.

Sophie had trouble keeping up with his long-legged strides as he hurried across the yard to the parked truck.

Mark slanted her a crooked smile. 'Could you feed the dogs and give them water?'

'Oh, sure.'

She hoped she didn't sound as stunned and nervous as she felt. Her experience with dogs was limited to her mother's toy poodle.

'Come to think of it,' Mark said, frowning, 'I'd better take Monty with me. I might need his help to keep the cattle in check. But I'll unchain Blue Dog and leave him with you. I'll feel better about leaving you here, if you have a dog about the place.'

'Why? Am I in real danger here?'

'Not with one of my dogs to keep an eye on you.'

That's not what I wanted to hear.

Scant minutes later, Sophie stood with her hands on her hips and with a blue-speckled cattle dog sitting at her heels.

'He's a working dog, so don't try to pat him,' Mark warned as he swung into the driver's seat.

Sophie cast a wary glance at Blue Dog's teeth. *Oh, help.* She was scared—of the dog, of the empty Outback, of being alone. 'Are you sure I wouldn't be any use if I came with you, Mark?'

He didn't hear her. Already he was slamming his door shut and revving the engine. With an elbow on the window sill, he leaned out.

'Why don't you check out my collection of DVDs? There should be something there to keep you entertained.'

With a wave, and a grin that made his teeth flash white in his brown face, he took off in a flurry of dust.

Blue Dog sat quietly beside Sophie, his tongue lolling as he panted, and the raw heat of the sun stung the back of her bare neck as she watched Mark hurry off down the rutted track without a backwards glance.

Hard to believe that half an hour ago she was being spoiled with breakfast in bed.

Sophie lost count of the number of times she went to the front veranda to look out, her hand shielding her eyes from the glare as she scoured the sunburnt paddocks, hoping to see a cloud of dust that meant Mark was on his way home.

She told herself that there was no need to be scared—not with Blue Dog sprawled across the front steps, his ears alert, his eyes watchful as he kept guard.

She didn't want to feel sorry for herself today. This was what happened in Mark's Outback, and if she was going to spend two weeks here she might as well try her level best to fit in. But she would not watch DVDs like a spoilt teenager, she would keep busy.

She found dried dog-food and put it in a bowl for Blue Dog, and poured water into another bowl. He lapped thirstily and then sank back into his sprawling pose across the top of the steps. He was a very quiet dog, not at all yappy, unlike her mother's poodle. It didn't seem right that she shouldn't pat him, but she caught another glimpse of those teeth and was quite happy to obey Mark.

Even though Mark's housekeeper had left meals, Sophie decided that apart from watering the pot plants on the veranda the only useful thing she could do was to cook. She loved cooking, and it might help to calm her frazzled nerves.

She turned on the radio for company, and to try to block out the disturbing silence of the vast, empty plains outside. She hunted through the enormous deep freeze in Mark's kitchen and found minced beef, so she made a huge lasagna. And a search of the pantry produced all the necessary ingredients for a traditional English sherry-trifle, so she made one of those, too.

With enough food to throw a party, she abandoned the kitchen and wandered through the house, picturing ways it could be improved with paint, curtains and attractive furniture.

She took her afternoon cup of tea onto the front veranda, so she could keep a lookout for Mark. But instead of Mark she saw a flock of large, ugly emus straggling across the stretch of dry grass in front of the homestead. Sophie watched them warily. The dog took no notice of them, but they were quite scary, with long legs, scraggy necks and fat bodies covered in untidy, dark-grey feathers.

Their eyes were fierce and staring, and their beaks strong and too sharply pointed for Sophie's liking. She waved her hands at them, trying to shoo them away, but they kept coming closer. She tried to remember what she'd heard about them. Were they vicious?

Her heart thrashed. Could they climb the front stairs? Could their ghastly beaks peck her to death? Terrified, she raced back inside the house and watched them through a window.

I hate this place!

Everything in the Outback was ugly and scary. Sophie fought back tears. She felt unbearably homesick for lovely green England with its hills of emerald velvet and its gentle valleys, its bluebell woods and pretty, babbling brooks.

Why on earth had she thought it was a good idea to come here?

The emus hung around for ages, but at last they wandered away. Relieved, Sophie was about to take a shower when the hot, still silence of the afternoon was broken by the shrill ring of the telephone.

Please let it be Mark. She tore through the house, and was a little breathless as she answered it.

'Hello, Sophie,' said a friendly voice. 'I'm Jill Jackson, Mark's neighbour.'

'Oh, hello!'

'I thought I'd ring to let you know that Mark is on his way home.'

Sinking thankfully onto a kitchen stool, Sophie said, 'That's good news, Jill. Thanks so much for letting me know.'

'Mark saved the day,' Jill said. 'The men would never have righted the truck without his help.'

'Really?' Sophie found that she was absurdly pleased. 'Then he's earned the nice dinner I've prepared for him.'

Jill laughed. 'I dare say he has.'

'I'm glad you rang.'

'My pleasure. I was pretty sure Mark wouldn't think to ring. The men were so preoccupied with a smashed-up road train and two hundred head of cattle that phone calls home wouldn't have scanned on their radar. But I know what it's like, waiting for news.'

'Thanks a lot. I appreciate it. Are you still there? At the crash?'

'Yes. I drove over at lunch time with extra provisions, but I'm heading home again now.'

Obviously, Jill was a proper Outback woman, the kind who pitched in with the men when necessary. Sophie squashed thoughts of inadequacy. She'd stayed back at the lonely homestead without a whimper, and that had been an act of courage as far as she was concerned.

'Andrew and I are hoping that you and Mark can come over for lunch,' Jill said. 'Actually, I've already mentioned it to Mark, and he suggested that Thursday would suit.'

'Oh? Well, yes, that would be lovely. Thank you.'

'I can't wait to meet you, Sophie.' Jill spoke with surprising warmth.

Sophie blinked. 'Really?'

'Mark's a wonderful neighbour. The nicest man I've ever known. Not counting Andrew, I suppose I should add.'

Sophie drew a shaky breath.

'We'll see you on Thursday, then?' enquired Jill.

'Yes,' Sophie assured her. 'I'm really looking forward to it.' But she couldn't help wondering what Mark had told his neighbours. What had he said that had caused the air of contained excitement in Jill's voice?

As soon as she heard the sound of a vehicle Sophie ran to the front veranda again, her eyes hungry for her first sight of Mark. She watched his truck roar up the track in a cloud of dust, saw the outline of his broad-brimmed hat and his wide shoulders, and her heart gave a very definite skip.

Mark waved, but kept driving around to the back of the house and came to a rattling stop under an enormous shade tree.

Blue Dog became a blurred streak, shooting down the steps and around the side of the house while Sophie followed at a more sedate pace. She watched Mark swing easily out of the truck and bend down to scratch the dog between his ears. 'Have you been a good guard dog?'

'He didn't move from the front steps,' Sophie announced as she drew near them.

Mark grinned at the dog, then looked up at her, and his face grew serious. 'How have you been?' he asked quietly.

'Fine.' She was determined that he mustn't guess how scared she'd been or how much she'd missed him.

'Good girl,' he said, in much the same tone that he

might say 'good dog', and then he straightened, took off his hat and ran his fingers through his dark hair. 'It's been a big day.'

Dinner that evening was very pleasant. Mark ate with clear enjoyment, and complimented Sophie's cooking many times. He told her about his day and about his neighbours, the Jacksons. Sophie wanted to ask him what he'd told them about her, but she decided to hold her tongue. Perhaps she'd misread Jill, and was making Mount Everest out of a molehill.

But as they carried the plates back to the kitchen she was rather surprised to see that Mark was frowning at her.

'What's the matter?' she asked.

'Tim rang this morning,' he said. 'He rang quite early, while you were still asleep, but then you were sick, and I was in such a rush to get away I decided not to mention it then.'

Sophie smacked a hand to her forehead. 'I forgot to ring Emma last night.' She'd been so caught up in events here that her friend had slipped her mind. 'I promised I'd ring to tell her I'd arrived safely. I suppose Tim was checking up on me.'

'Well, yes, he was asking about you. He knows about the baby.'

'Emma told him. I had to confide in her, Mark. She's my best friend.'

He nodded. 'Tim gave me quite a lecture. Carried on about what a sweet little thing you are.'

'Naturally.' Sophie tossed a coy smile over her shoulder as she rinsed their plates at the sink.

Mark said quietly, but with a disturbing undertone, 'He mentioned your boyfriend.'

'Oliver?' Sophie's smile vanished. She still couldn't say that name without feeling sick. 'He's my ex,' she said stiffly. 'But I don't see why Tim needed to mention him.'

Leaning against a kitchen cupboard, Mark folded his arms and regarded her from beneath slightly hooded, unreadable eyes.

Sophie squirmed. 'I suppose Tim told you how we broke up?'

'He said you were about to announce your engagement when the boyfriend suddenly called it off.'

She nodded.

'Sounds like a nasty type.'

'Oliver's a rat,' she said vehemently.

'Oliver?' Mark's frown deepened. 'Wasn't there a guy called Oliver at the wedding—a tall, fair-haired fellow?'

'Yes.'

His eyes narrowed. 'He had a fiancée dangling on his arm, didn't he? I remember there were people making quite a fuss.'

Sophie's stomach lurched uncomfortably, and she gripped the edge of the sink. Mark would think she was such a loser.

'Don't tell me that Oliver guy at the wedding was your ex?'

Feeling sick, Sophie nodded. She turned to check Mark's expression. Too late, she realised where this conversation was heading.

'I don't suppose,' he said with menacing quiet, 'old Oliver was the reason you were so keen to dance with *me?*'

Sophie flinched, suddenly hypnotised by the dawning

anger in Mark's eyes. She knew she had to defend herself, but her tongue was glued to the roof of her mouth.

'You might have warned me you were on the rebound,' he said.

'But I—'

'It might have been fair to let me know that I was ammunition for your counter attack. I would have appreciated knowing that you flirted with me and danced with me, and *slept* with me, simply because you needed to snub Oliver.'

She wanted to cry, '*No, no, no!*'

But what was the point of lying when Mark had already worked out the truth?

Except…except he only had half the truth.

Nevertheless, guilt flooded Sophie. She didn't dare to look at Mark. She stared at the floor while her heart began a panicky dance. With every moment that she spent with Mark, she liked him more—really liked him—in spite of his Outback. And she hoped that he liked her.

Deep down, she nursed a secret hope that they might find a way to make their relationship work. But if she couldn't allay Mark's doubts she might as well pack her bags and head straight back to London now.

Bravely, she lifted her head to meet his burning black gaze. 'I'll admit I started flirting with you to show Oliver that he hadn't hurt me.'

Mark remained very still with his arms tightly crossed over his chest, his face a dark, inscrutable mask. 'I need to check on the dogs,' he said quietly, and he turned to leave.

'But I haven't finished, Mark. You need to understand. My feelings were very mixed up that night, but when I—'

'Don't make it worse,' he snapped. 'I understand perfectly.' And then he shoved the flyscreen door open and strode out into the black of the night.

Sophie ran after him, batting blindly at the flyscreen door and letting it slam behind her, but when she got to the veranda she stopped. She desperately wanted to follow him, but beyond the house it was dark.

Already Mark had disappeared.

Oh, help. There were snakes and spiders out there that she wouldn't be able to see. And somewhere out in the dark paddocks there was a dreadful bird that kept making a blood-curdling, mournful cry like a distraught mother crying for a dead child.

'Mark, wait!'

His voice came out of the darkness. 'Do me a favour, Sophie. Stay inside.'

He spoke with such deep, quiet authority that she knew this was an order. It was not the time to confront Mark.

She had no choice but to stay in the safe, brightly lit kitchen and wait for him to come back inside.

Sick at heart, she stacked the dishwasher, then made a pot of tea and drank two cups. But Mark didn't come back.

Sophie knew he was avoiding her. He obviously had a stubborn streak and a great deal of pride, and she could hear him out in one of the sheds, tinkering with machinery. Eventually she understood there was no point in trying to talk this through tonight.

Feeling utterly miserable, she gave up waiting and went to bed. She could only hope that in the morning Mark would be prepared to listen.

CHAPTER SIX

THE phone rang again next morning, just as Mark came into the kitchen. He'd slept badly, and wasn't in the mood for phone calls, and he snatched it up angrily.

'Good morning.'

'Is that Coolabah Waters?'

The caller was a woman with a rich, mature and highly cultured English accent. Fine hairs lifted on the back of Mark's neck. Almost certainly the woman was calling Sophie, but, judging by the ominous sounds he'd heard when he'd passed the bathroom just now, she was in the grip of morning sickness.

'Yes,' he said carefully. 'This is Mark Winchester speaking.'

'Eliza Felsham here, Mark. I believe my daughter, Sophie, may have visited you recently.'

Something brick-shaped lodged in Mark's throat. He'd been mentally preparing himself for an awkward conversation with Sophie's father at some stage in the future, but her mother was another matter entirely. He swallowed. 'Sophie's still here, Lady Eliza. I—I imagine you'd like to speak to her?'

'Yes, please. But, before you go, there are a few

questions I'd like to ask you.' The imperious voice made him squirm like a schoolboy summoned to the head-mistress's office.

'Certainly.' Mark hoped his grimace didn't show in his voice. He took a deep breath. 'What would you like to know?'

He braced himself for the worst.

Is it true that you've impregnated my precious daughter? Haven't you heard of safe sex in Australia?

'Where exactly in Australia do you live, Mark?'

The unexpected question caught him flat-footed, and he wished he could clear his throat. 'I have a cattle property in north-western Queensland.'

'What's the name of the nearest town?'

'Wandabilla.'

'Wanda *what*?' Lady Eliza demanded. 'How do you spell that?'

Patiently, Mark told her.

'Hmm…that doesn't show here. Could you tell me the nearest good-sized city?'

Mark suppressed an uneasy sigh. Lady Eliza's prima-donna qualities were certainly coming to the fore. 'The nearest town of note would be Mount Isa.' He heard the rustle of pages in the background, as if Sophie's mother was searching through an atlas.

'Ah, yes, I've found it,' she said. 'Good heavens.' There was an unnervingly long beat of silence. 'You must be very isolated.'

Mark forced a smile into his voice. 'Coolabah Waters is remote, but don't worry about your daughter's safety, Lady Eliza. She's—' he inhaled sharply '—in good hands.'

'I'm very pleased to hear that, Mark.' Her tone was surprisingly pleasant.

'I'll get Sophie.'

'Thank you.'

He hurried down the hallway to the bathroom and knocked on the door. 'Sophie?' he called carefully.

There was no reply. No doubt she was upset with him, after last night.

'Sophie!' Mark called more loudly, and his heart began an echoing knock against his ribs as he imagined the excuses he would have to offer Lady Eliza if her daughter wasn't well enough to come to the phone.

But to his relief the door opened and Sophie appeared, looking pale and tired, as if she hadn't slept.

'Your mother's on the phone,' he told her.

She groaned and closed her eyes, but almost immediately her eyes flashed open again. 'Does she know about the baby?'

Mark lifted his hands helplessly. 'She didn't mention it to me.'

'I begged Emma not to tell her.'

'I don't think she knows. She doesn't sound upset, but she's waiting. You can take the call in my study, if you like. I'll hang up the phone in the kitchen.'

Sophie felt several versions of rotten as she made her way to the study. The continuing effects of jet lag, morning sickness and Mark's horrible reaction after dinner last night had been a lethal combination.

Gingerly, she lifted the receiver. 'Hello, Mum. How are you?'

'I'm perfectly fine, darling. Just a little surprised, of course. I didn't expect to get back from Milan and find a garbled message on my phone telling me you've taken off for Australia on a holiday. That was a sudden decision, wasn't it?'

'Well, yes, it was a bit.'

'You left no information except this one telephone number, Sophie. Are you all right, dear? You sound a little…flat.'

'I'm fine, Mum.' Sophie injected extra brightness into her voice. 'Brilliant, actually.'

'That's good to hear.' After a pause, 'So how long are you staying at Mark Winchester's cattle property?'

After last night, she wasn't sure how she stood with Mark, but she said, 'About two weeks.'

This was greeted by unpromising silence. And then, 'When did you meet this young man, darling?'

'A couple of months ago.' Sophie tried to sound breezy and cool. 'At Emma and Tim's wedding. Mark was Tim's best man.'

'Oh, I see.' Her mother's tone was instantly lighter, and indicated that she saw much more than Sophie would have liked her to. 'So Mark's a good friend of Tim's, obviously.'

'That's right.'

There was a distinct sigh of relief. 'I'm sure he must be a fine young man, then.'

A coy chuckle on the other end of the line startled Sophie. She swallowed her gasp of surprise.

'I must say, Mark has the most marvellous voice, Sophie. A very rich baritone. Almost a bass.'

'Yes, it is deep.'

'I imagine he must be very tall?'

'Quite tall.'

'And dark?'

'Yes, Mum.'

To Sophie's alarm, her mother let out a sound that was suspiciously close to a dreamy sigh. 'It was such a pity that your father and I had to go to Sweden and miss the wedding. I must ring Emma and ask to see her photos.'

Sophie winced. Now her mother was getting disturbingly excited, almost as if she could hear another set of wedding bells in the air. 'Mum, Mark and I are—are just friends.'

'Yes, dear. Of course. And his Outback cattle property is so interesting that you don't want to bother with any of the sights in Australia—Sydney or Uluru or the Great Barrier Reef?'

'I—I don't have enough money to visit all those expensive tourist-spots.'

After a pause, Lady Eliza asked, 'Are there many people living on Coolabah Waters? I understand that some of those big properties have huge numbers of staff.'

'Umm.' Sophie's hand felt suddenly slick with sweat, and she almost dropped the telephone receiver. 'Mark has a caretaker, but—' She cast a frantic glance to the doorway, but Mark had disappeared. 'But he's had to go away.'

'How inconvenient.' Eliza's voice rippled with a complicated blend of concern and innuendo. 'So you and Mark are spending two weeks alone?'

'More—more or less.'

'Sophie, darling, you are being sensible, aren't you?'

'Of course, Mum.'

'You're such a warm, impulsive little thing. I'd hate you to break your heart again.'

'Don't worry about me. I'm being super-sensible. And I'll be home again before you know it.'

To her surprise, her mother seemed willing to leave it at that. 'All right, then. I won't be a bore and make a fuss. So I suppose there's not much for me to say, except enjoy yourself, my dear.'

'I will. Thanks for calling, Mum. Give my love to Dad.'

'Yes, yes. Stay safe, darling.'

As soon as Sophie hung up, she slumped in the chair beside Mark's desk. Until this morning, she'd pushed her parents out of her mind. But now she could picture her mother's intelligent, beautiful face, could hear her relaying this phone conversation to her father. Sir Kenneth would not be so easily mollified, and he certainly wouldn't be won over by Mark's smooth, dark, baritone voice.

To make matters worse, Sophie knew that as soon as her mother saw photos of Mark, looking so handsome and splendid in his best man's suit, she would be convinced that her daughter had fallen head-over-heels in love with him. And she would quiz poor Emma.

And Emma knew about the baby.

Oh, help!

Sophie jumped from the chair in sudden panic and hurried down the hallway to the kitchen. 'Mark?'

He was doing something with a frying pan at the stove, and he turned as she hurried into the room. 'Everything all right?' he asked.

'On the surface,' she said with an uncertain shrug.

'Does your mother know—about the baby?'

'Not yet. But I'll have to ring Emma, to warn her to be ready for a call.'

'That's fine. Go ahead.'

Mark was polite enough, but he still spoke with an edge of reserve that chilled Sophie. As she returned to the study and dialled Emma's number, she wished she felt more confident about her chances of convincing him that she hadn't just used him to get back at Oliver.

But how hard would it be to convince him? She'd known from the start that there was something very strong and rock solid about Mark, a kind of unfailing inner strength, but that probably meant he was also very stubborn.

Emma's number was engaged. 'Damn,' Sophie said softly. 'I wonder if Mum's already called her.' After a panicky moment, she decided she would have to try Emma's mobile. You never knew, she might answer it even if she was taking another call.

She dialled, and chewed her lip as she waited.

Emma's voice said, 'Hello?'

Sophie let out a huff of relief. 'Emma, it's Sophie.'

'Sophie? What a coincidence. I'm in the middle of a phone conversation with your mother.'

'Oh, she beat me to it. I was hoping to warn you. Is she grilling you about Mark?'

'And how.'

Sophie nodded sympathetically. 'You won't tell her, will you? About the baby?'

'Trust me, Sox. I won't spill the beans. But I'd better hurry back. I'm in the middle of telling Lady E how dashing and gorgeous and marriageable your Mark is.'

'But why? There's no talk of us getting married!'

'Well, that's a jolly shame,' Emma remarked unhelpfully.

Sophie felt only marginally better as she hung up. She

imagined Emma and her mother gossiping madly about her, and she pressed her hands over her mouth to hold back a groan. Very soon her father and sisters would all know about Mark. They would be certain Sophie was madly in love with him. Why else would she have dashed to the other side of the world to be with him?

And, after the fiasco with Oliver, they would be on tenterhooks, half expecting her to end up with a broken heart again. Another failure.

And, unless she could redress last night's misunderstanding, she knew that was exactly where she was heading.

Mark's sausages and tomatoes were almost burned black, but he stayed at the stove, wrestling with his thoughts.

He'd been rattled ever since last night's revelation. Until then, he'd assumed that Sophie had come all this way because she fancied him, because she hoped to make a go of their relationship. Poor fool that he was, he'd allowed himself to imagine that they'd both shared a similar instant attraction at the wedding.

He'd thought a lot about it last night, nursing his ego as he'd tinkered uselessly with the old tractor in the shed.

Now, he realised he hadn't a clue how Sophie really felt, and it disturbed him more than it probably should to know that he'd been part of a payback manoeuvre. A payback manoeuvre that had misfired.

And how it had misfired! Sophie's pregnancy had to be the worst possible result.

On top of that, Tim and Emma and Lady Eliza Felsham were all worried that she would be hurt again. Man, talk about pressure on him.

Problem was, he'd fallen halfway in love with a woman who probably had no interest in him apart from the child they'd accidentally conceived.

And yet, he couldn't help feeling sorry for Sophie, couldn't help wanting to protect her.

Getting this right was like walking a tightrope, and Mark was damn sure he didn't want to put a foot wrong. He had to make clear decisions with his head, not his heart. He had to set aside the romantic notion that he could woo Sophie over the next two weeks, had to ignore her tempting little mouth, her delectable body.

He had to remember that she wouldn't want to live here anyway. His mission had to be to take the best possible care of her and send her home in two weeks' time with a secure promise of regular contact and financial support.

Until then he would keep her safe.

They ate in uncomfortable silence.

Sophie waited until Mark had finished his breakfast before she tried to take up where they'd left off last night. She'd had a lot of time to think about what she had to say, but she still wasn't sure that when she opened her mouth the right words would come out.

Butterflies fluttered in her stomach as she watched Mark drain the last of his coffee and set the cup down.

His expression was carefully blank as he looked at her. 'I thought you might like to take a tour over parts of the property today. If you're feeling up to it, that is.'

She took a deep breath, and spread her hands flat on the table. 'Before we talk about that, there's something else more important that I want to set straight.'

His throat worked. 'What is it?' He dropped his gaze, and began to gather up his breakfast things.

'Look at me, please, Mark.'

His hands stopped moving. Very slowly, he lifted his head, and Sophie's heart began to thump when she saw that all warmth had drained from his face.

I have to get this right. I can't make another mistake.

'You have to believe me,' she said. 'It's true that I started flirting with you at the wedding to get back at Oliver. But my decision to invite you back to my flat had nothing to do with Oliver. It was all about you.'

Nervously she reached out and touched the back of his hand with her fingertips. 'The only thing that influenced me to sleep with you was how I felt about you. I didn't give Oliver a single thought. It was all about you, Mark.'

When he didn't protest, she hurried on more confidently. 'You were far too dashing and handsome, Mark. I was totally smitten. A girl didn't stand a chance with you kitted out in your best-man's finery.'

He was looking deep into her eyes now.

Oh, please let him see that I'm telling the truth!

She held her breath.

Slowly, slowly, a faint glimmer stirred the darkness in his eyes. His upper lip curled as if he was fighting hard not to smile. At last, he said, 'So the expensive suit I hired did the trick?'

'I promise. You were a knockout, Mr Winchester.'

'Touché,' he said softly. 'You were far too lovely in your pretty bridesmaid's gown.'

'Really?'

'Oh, yeah.'

His smile came fully then, warming his whole face,

making his eyes shine with a glow that caused a clutch in Sophie heart. She drew a deep breath of relief. Mark did the same.

Yesterday, they might have fallen into each other's arms. Today they were more cautious.

Mark simply stood, but his tread was lighter as he took his dishes to the sink. 'About this tour of the property,' he said. 'Are you interested?'

If Mark had asked that question when she'd first arrived, Sophie might have been content with a tame tour over Coolabah Waters. But ever since Jill's phone call, she'd been hoping to become more involved in the day-to-day life on his cattle property. She wanted to impress him, needed to prove that she could fit in.

'Are you sure you have time for a sightseeing tour?' she asked. 'What about your work? You've been away for a couple of weeks, and I'm sure you must have oodles to do.'

His eyebrows lifted in surprise. 'There are fences that need fairly urgent attention,' he admitted. 'But a fencing job would take me most of the day. It would mean abandoning you again.'

'Why can't I come, too?'

Mark couldn't have looked more surprised if she'd announced that she wanted to walk across the Simpson Desert barefoot. 'It's too hot out there, Sophie. You'd hate it.'

'I've been outside. It's not that bad. I'd like to come.'

'But you're pregnant,' he protested.

'That doesn't mean I'm made of porcelain.'

'You were sick again this morning,' he added faintly. 'And I promised your mother I'd take good care of you.'

'I'm feeling fine now, Mark. I'd like to come.'

He sighed.

Hands on hips, Sophie eyed him levelly. 'I'm not a snowflake in the desert. I'm prepared to give your Outback a go.'

He cast a cautious glance over her clothes—denim shorts and a sleeveless cotton top.

'You couldn't go out dressed like that. That lovely skin of yours would be burned to a crisp in ten minutes out there. You'll have to cover up. Do you have jeans and a long-sleeved shirt?'

'I brought jeans, but none of my shirts have long sleeves.'

'You'll have to borrow one of mine, then. You can roll the sleeves up and wear it loose over the top—just to keep the sun off.'

Sophie was so pleased that Mark had stopped fighting her objections, she would have worn a tent.

He looked down at her dainty white sandals covered in daisies. 'Do you have anything sturdier to put on your feet?'

'Would sneakers do?'

'They'll have to. What about a hat?'

'I brought a sunhat with me.'

'A decent one with a wide brim?'

'Well, the brim's not terribly wide. I needed something I could squash into my suitcase. But if I unpick the daisies—'

Mark laughed. 'Forget it. You'd better wear one of my hats, too. It might not be pretty, but it will save your complexion.'

* * *

Half an hour later, she was grateful for Mark's big blue, double-pocket cotton shirt and his hat with a brim as wide as a veranda. She was standing in the middle of an enormous brown paddock with a fierce sun beating down, while she watched Mark pace out a line for metal fence-posts that he called star pickets.

To Sophie, the pickets looked rather thin and insubstantial—nothing like the old stone walls and strong timber fences on the farms she'd seen in England.

'Why don't you use timber?' she asked.

'The white ants would eat timber posts in no time,' he said as he pulled on leather gloves and began to lift heavy rolls of barbed wire from the back of the ute. 'We use timber from special termite-resistant trees for the gate posts and strainers, but otherwise these are best.'

'Do you have to look after all your fences?' There seemed to be thousands of miles of them.

'I use contract fencers for the big jobs. This is just a small maintenance job of a few hundred metres.'

'A bit like me changing a light bulb at home,' she joked.

Mark's white teeth flashed as he grinned.

'So, what can I do to help?'

She was pleased that he only hesitated briefly before he handed her a pair of gloves.

'You'd be a great help if you could hold the pickets steady, so I can ram them in. Keep your hands away from the top, and hold the picket about halfway down.'

'Right.'

She crouched to hold the slim black post in place, while Mark used a heavy-capped metal pipe with two handles that fitted over the picket.

He lifted the post driver a foot or so, then slammed the pipe down, forcing the picket into the ground with each blow.

'Much easier than driving it in with a sledgehammer,' he grunted.

Sophie thought it still looked like jolly hard work as she watched Mark's shirt stretch tightly over his broad shoulders, threatening to split.

His shirt tail lifted, exposing a glimpse of bare skin at his waist.

This is why he has such a great body, she thought, admiring his trim hips, strong thighs and wonderful biceps. He did this sort of hard work all the time. No need for a gym workout for this man.

He swung around and she quickly switched her gaze to the ute, but she knew he'd caught her checking him out.

'Ready with the next one?' he called.

'Sure.'

They worked their way along the fence line and, once the pickets were in place, Mark tensioned the wire with a metal lever, a bit like an old-fashioned tyre jack.

Sophie couldn't drag her eyes from him. His movements were so practised, so easy and fluid and unhurried, and yet he conveyed the capacity to be very quick indeed if it was necessary.

As the fence took shape, she felt a completely unwarranted sense of achievement. OK, so maybe her help had been minimal, but she thought they made a pretty good team.

They lunched in the shade of gum trees, enjoying sandwiches and tea from the flask. Mark found an old blanket in the ute and spread it on the grass.

'You should have a little rest before we head back,' he said.

In no mood to argue, she stretched out and looked up at the sky through the tree branches. It was astonishingly blue and clear. There wasn't a cloud anywhere.

'A granddad sky,' she said, speaking her thoughts aloud.

'I beg your pardon?' Mark was sitting with his back against a tree trunk and his long legs stretched in front of him, and he regarded her with quizzical amusement.

'Whenever I see a perfectly clear, blue sky without any clouds, I think of my grandfather. We don't get too many perfectly spotless blue skies in England. But when I was quite small I was out in the country walking with Grandad and we saw a perfect, clear sky.'

She pointed. 'Deep blue. Just like this. And he told me if I ever saw another sky better than that I was to write and tell him.'

'And will you?'

'I can't. He died two years ago.'

Mark's eyes were sympathetic. 'He sounds like a nice fellow.'

'He was. The best.' She watched a flock of brightly coloured little birds swoop down to perch in a small tree to her right.

'I think Grandad and I were the odd ones out in our family,' she said. 'Whenever he came to my mother's Sunday lunch-parties, he got as bored as I did with all the music gossip, so we usually slipped away. Sometimes we'd just go into the garden to peak into birds' nests, or hunt for hedgehogs, but other times we'd sneak up to the High Street. He'd let me stuff myself silly with cream cakes and he'd never tell my mother.'

Mark chuckled, and Sophie rolled onto her side so she could see him better. 'The summer before Grandad died, I took him up to Scotland. I sat on a river bank for hours, reading novels, while he fished for trout to his heart's content.'

'Every man should be so lucky.'

A kind of shadow came over his face, and he sighed. 'My father died five years ago, fighting a bushfire. He worked hard all his life. I wish I'd thought to take him on a holiday.'

'Perhaps he was happy to be living in the bush on a beautiful property.'

'Yeah. Perhaps.' He sent her a grateful smile. 'Dad and Mum were very close. She died eighteen months later. They called it heart failure, but I think she missed him too much.'

'That's very sweet, really.' A painful lump filled Sophie's throat as she thought of Mark's parents living a self-contained, happy life in the Outback. Together and very much in love.

As she lay there, lost in a romantic fantasy where she was the next Mrs Winchester, she rubbed her tummy in an absentminded, careless kind of way.

Watching her, Mark said, 'I wonder if the baby's a boy or a girl.'

'Have you been thinking about that?' she asked, surprised.

'Sure. Haven't you?'

'I haven't dared,' she admitted.

'You mean you haven't been playing around, trying out names?'

'No.'

'I thought all women liked to do that.'

She closed her eyes. 'It would make being pregnant all too real.'

'But it is real, Sophie.'

Mark sounded shocked, and her eyes flashed open. She looked directly at him. His dark eyes were very serious, almost intimidating.

What she hadn't said was that thinking up names for the baby would have involved trusting the future, and Oliver had spoiled her ability to do that.

'I—I just think of it as my little bean,' she said.

'Bean?'

'Well, yes. Because it's just a little thing, a little blob, curled like a bean.'

His expression softened. 'A human bean?'

'Yes,' Sophie said, and her mouth began to twitch. 'A little human bean. Our little human bean.'

A helpless chuckle broke from her.

Next moment, Mark was grinning, too. Their gazes met, and Sophie felt quite overcome by the sense of connection she felt with him. After their morning working together, she dared to wonder for the first time if she and Mark might still be together when the baby was born.

It was a thought almost too big to take in. She pulled Mark's hat over her face, and tried to calm down by listening to the sun-drowsed stillness of the Outback.

The silence didn't disturb her as much today. She no longer missed the background hum of traffic and city sounds, and she was able to enjoy the peacefulness.

She lay very still and let her shoulders, then her whole body, relax. The only sound was the faint buzz of insects in the grass and her soft breathing. She was aware of the faint puffs of air passing from her nostrils and over her upper lip. And as she lay there, thinking about the sky and the tapering blue-green gum trees, her breath drifting slowly in and out, she felt for a fleeting moment connected to the entire universe.

She must have fallen asleep then, because she woke with a start when she heard Mark moving about, packing their things into the back of the ute.

She sat up stiffly. 'Have I been asleep long?'

He smiled. 'About an hour.'

'Heavens! Just as well I'm not being paid by the hour.'

He held up the flask. 'Would you like the last of the tea?'

'Thanks. It might help me to wake up.'

As Mark handed her the metal cup, she saw that he'd stowed everything away and that grey shadows had begun to stretch from the trees out across the newly mended fence and the yellowed grass.

They started back to the homestead in the cool of the afternoon, and as the shadows lengthened families of kangaroos came out to graze.

'If you like, I'll show you how to stalk right up to kangaroos,' he said. 'If you freeze every time they look up from feeding, you can almost get close enough to touch them.'

Sophie grinned. 'Sounds like fun.'

She couldn't believe how relaxed she felt. The bush wasn't nearly so scary with Mark beside her, his hands expertly guiding their vehicle around a huge anthill, then letting the wheel spin free as he corrected their direction and rushed on over the trackless ground.

She decided there was something almost infallible

about Mark Winchester in this environment. His quiet competence put her completely at ease, and she knew she could trust him.

Until he said suddenly, 'If we're supposed to be getting to know each other better, why don't you tell me more about Oliver?'

CHAPTER SEVEN

SOPHIE'S sense of peace deserted her. Was she never to be free of the spectre of Oliver? 'What do you want to know?' she asked nervously.

Mark stared grimly ahead through the windscreen. 'You were going to marry the man. You must have loved him.'

She winced. She hated having to relive the humiliation of Oliver's rejection. But she supposed it was best to be completely honest with Mark. If she got this out in the open, she might with luck be able to leave it behind.

'I did love Oliver,' she admitted unhappily. 'At least, I thought I did. He's an accomplished musician, and I was flattered when he took an interest in me. And I suppose I thought my parents would be pleased.'

'Were they?'

'Not as pleased as I'd hoped.' Sophie fiddled nervously with her hair, winding a curl around her forefinger and then letting it spring free, before grabbing it again. 'I didn't realise he was a rat until it was too late.' She bit her lip.

Mark frowned at her. 'Too late?'

Sophie stopped fiddling with her hair and straightened her spine, summoned the dignity necessary to get through this confession. 'It wasn't until after I agreed to marry Oliver that I discovered he was only dating me because of my family.'

The shocked look on Mark's face was comforting. It reminded her of the night they'd met, when his refusal to be excessively impressed by her clever relations had endeared him to her.

'Oliver fancies himself as a concert master,' she explained. 'And a composer. Actually, minimalist opera is his big thing. He adored my mother.'

'Minimalist opera? What the hell is that?'

She rolled her eyes. 'Act one, a guy feels a sneeze coming on. Act two, he puts his hand in his pocket and pulls out a handkerchief. Act three, he sneezes.'

Mark's eyebrows rose high. 'Then dies?'

'No, dying only happens in grand opera.'

Chuckling, he shook his head, clearly bewildered by the entire concept.

'Oliver hoped that by marrying me he could convince my father to boost him into a brilliant career. But Dad wasn't very impressed with him, and, as soon as Oliver realised that his dreams were toast, he dumped me.'

Mark's hands tightened on the steering wheel. 'That must have been very rough.'

She lifted one shoulder in a carefully nonchalant shrug. 'For a time there, it wasn't pleasant.'

To her relief, Mark didn't press her for more details. They drove on in silence, while the sky in the west began to fade to the palest blue streaked with pink.

When she felt a little calmer, Sophie said, 'Should I

be enquiring about your girlfriends, Mark? Is there anyone special?'

He smiled and shook his head. 'I've been so busy since I bought this place, I haven't had time for a social life.'

'I take it you haven't always lived here?'

'No. I grew up on Wynstead, a much prettier property near the coast, and after my father died I took over the running of it.'

'Why did you come out here, then?' She couldn't help asking this. A prettier property near the coast sounded so much more appealing.

'I wanted to expand. These days you either have to get big or get out. I didn't want to leave the cattle industry, so I hired a manager for Wynstead and came further west to more marginal country. The land's cheaper out here, but you need much more of it. I can run thousands of head of cattle, but it's a harder life.'

'How long have you been here?'

'A little over a year. I'm still in the process of knocking the property into shape.'

Sophie sank back into her seat as she digested this. It explained why Mark hadn't done anything about his dingy and depressing house. She found it interesting that he was something of a pioneer, prepared to put up with hardship in the short term while planning for a brighter future.

'I'm glad you let me come fencing today,' she said. 'But I still feel as if I have no idea about the things you normally do. I haven't seen any of your cowboy antics. I haven't seen you on a horse. I—I haven't even patted a cow.'

His eyes widened. 'You want to pat a cow?'

'Um—well—' Sophie imagined getting close to one

of those enormous, multi-hoofed animals and made a quick adjustment. 'Maybe I could start with something less daunting—like one of your dogs?'

His lips twitched. 'I told you, my cattle dogs are working dogs. They might try to take off your fingers.'

'Oh.' *Well, that puts me in my place!*

'But they'd let you pat them if I told them it was OK.'

'That's big of them. I do find that a full set of fingers is rather useful.'

They came to a pair of metal gates between two paddocks. Mark stopped the vehicle, jumped out, opened the gates and then climbed back in.

Sophie shot him a thoughtful frown. 'If I was a proper Outback girl I'd open and close those gates for you, wouldn't I?'

He shrugged as he shoved the gear stick into first. 'Perhaps. But it's not necessary.'

'Let me close them,' she said, thrusting her door open.

'You don't have to, Sophie.'

'I want to!'

Didn't Mark understand? She didn't want to be treated like an English tourist. She would never fit into life in the Outback if she was constantly mollycoddled. Jumping to the ground, she gave him a jaunty wave, and he drove the truck through, then she swung the gate closed and hurried to lock it.

She'd seen Mark doing this before. It was dead easy. All she had to do was pull a chain through the gate and loop it over a bolt on the stout timber fence-post.

An impossibly big bolt.

No way could she stretch the metal chain to loop over it. Three times she tried and failed. *Darn.* Sophie refrained from stamping her foot, and she didn't dare to look back to Mark, couldn't bear to see his knowing smirk. If he made a wisecrack, so help her, she might box his ears. There had to be a trick to this. Perhaps she was trying too hard.

If she took this more slowly, lifted the chain higher and—

'Here.' Mark's deep voice sounded beside her. 'Let me show you.'

She looked up, her chin stubbornly proud. She didn't want his assistance. She'd helped him with fencing, so surely she could do something as simple as shut a gate!

But, although Mark was smiling, she saw to her relief that he was not making fun of her. His big hands closed over hers. 'There's a bit of a trick to it,' he said gently. 'You need to tilt the chain like so.'

Naturally, when he did it the chain slipped easily over the bolt.

'If you'd given me another minute, I would have worked that out,' she protested.

'Of course you would have.' Mark smiled again and let his knuckles gently graze the side of her cheek.

Her skin burned at his touch, and her heart skittered like a frisky colt. 'I'll be all right with the next gate.'

'Sure.'

Mark dropped his hand, and she let out a shaky breath as they climbed back into the ute.

They continued on in charged silence until Mark said, 'I didn't realise you wanted a really close encounter with Outback life.'

'But I'm supposed to be getting to know you better,'

she said defensively. 'Shouldn't that involve getting to know about the everyday things you usually do? I mean, I don't even know what you do when you look after your cattle.'

He gave her a quick glance. 'I suppose you want a few details so you can tell our child about me when he's older?'

'Well…yes.' She felt suddenly, unaccountably depressed.

Ever since their conversation about the bean, she'd been toying with the romantic possibility that she could morph miraculously into a woman of the Outback, that she and Mark could really make a relationship work.

But it was jolly obvious that her thoughts were racing way ahead of Mark's. He was sticking to their original plan, and he fully expected her to go straight back to England at the end of next week to raise their child alone.

It was crazy to get carried away with dreams of something else. She'd known all along that there was no point in falling for Mark, or starting to weave dreams about living here. He wanted what was best for the baby, but today she'd learned that he was also struggling to get this property on its feet. An Englishwoman and a tiny baby were added burdens he could do without.

Unfortunately.

When they got back to the homestead, the blue-speckled cattle dogs barked a noisy greeting from their kennels beneath the shady mango tree. Mark climbed down from the ute and gave them a playful scuff about the ears, and then he looked back at Sophie. 'Would you like to say hello?'

Her enthusiasm for a close encounter with the Outback had dimmed somewhat on the journey back, but she put on a brave face and gave the dogs a self-conscious wave. 'Hi, guys.'

'Come and meet them properly,' Mark said, offering her a sideways grin.

Her hands had automatically clenched behind her back, and she kept them there as she took a couple of steps closer.

'Monty, Blue Dog, this is Sophie,' Mark announced rather grandly. 'I want you two to say hello to her very nicely.'

The dogs quieted immediately and stood looking up at Sophie, their intelligent eyes watchful, their pointy ears alert, tails wagging more sedately.

'You can pat them now,' Mark said, watching her with mild amusement.

Sophie tried to unclench her hands from behind her back. *Me and my big mouth.* Mark might have given permission, but the dogs still had frighteningly big teeth! And their short hair looked rather bristly.

'I'm actually more of a cat person,' she said, to show that she wasn't completely out of touch with the animal world.

But she took a tiny step towards Blue Dog—after all, he'd looked after her so beautifully yesterday.

Fortune favours the brave.

She held out her hand, preparing to deliver a swift pat on his head, but to her amazement the dog sat and lifted a paw to her.

'He wants to shake hands?' She shot Mark a look of amazed delight, and her nervousness melted as she bent down and took the dog's paw. 'Hello, Blue Dog.'

She rather liked the feel of the soft pad of his paw,

upholstered with work-toughened skin. And, when she patted the fur between his ears, she discovered that it was soft and quite pleasant to touch. Not bristly at all.

The introduction was repeated with Monty.

'They are so impressive, Mark.' Hands on hips, Sophie turned to him, beaming with unabashed admiration. 'How did you get them to do that?'

'Hand signals,' he replied airily. 'Now, show me *your* hand.'

Puzzled, she held it out to him, and her heart stumbled as he took her rather small, white hand and cradled it in his hands, which were by contrast very big and brown.

Sophie struggled to breathe as Mark examined her fingers. He turned her hand over gently and then back again, touching her knuckles, her fingertips, one by one. It was quite unfair of him, really. Didn't he know that electricity zapped through her whenever he touched her?

'W-what are you doing?' she stammered.

His face was close to hers, and when she looked up she found herself looking directly into his dark-brown eyes. 'I'm making sure you haven't lost a finger,' he said, and his slow smile made her insides roll like a tumbleweed.

'Now,' he said, letting her hand go, and apparently quite unaware that he'd reduced her to a puddle of melted hormones. 'Would you like to come with me while I take a look at the horses?'

Sophie gulped. 'I—I suppose it won't hurt to work my way up the animal kingdom.'

The horses weren't kept in stables, but in a long, skinny paddock that stretched from the stockyards beside the barn down to a string of trees lining an almost-dry creek bed. As they approached the fence line, Mark put his little fingers to the corners of his mouth and let out a shrill whistle. The horses were at the far end of the paddock, but they all turned together like choreographed dancers and began to canter gracefully over the yellow grass towards them.

One glance at Mark and Sophie could see that he was very fond and proud of these creatures, and she had to admit they were rather gorgeous in a scary, long-legged and horsy kind of way.

There were four of them in a mixture of colours— dappled grey, chestnut, piebald and black.

Mark went forward to greet them as they came up to the fence, but Sophie stood well back, her hands once more tightly clasped behind her back. Patting dogs was one thing, but horses were another matter entirely. To start with, they had much bigger teeth!

But she'd claimed that she wanted to know all about Outback life, and she couldn't exactly change her mind now.

Reaching up, Mark patted one horse's neck, and stroked the nose of another. He smiled at her again. 'This is Tilly. She's very gentle. Come and say hello.'

Tilly was the chestnut, rather pretty, with a white blaze on her forehead and a silky black mane. But gentle? Sophie eyed the mare's arched neck, her raised tail and wrinkled lips revealing very large teeth. She didn't think gentleness was a possibility.

'Horses don't bite, do they, Mark?'

His eyes flashed as he grinned back at her. 'These are OK, but some stallions can be nasty. I'd rather be bitten by a dog than a horse any day.'

'I might say hello from here,' she said. But she could hear how wimpy and wet that sounded, and she forced herself to take a quick step forward. But, good grief, the closer she got to the horse the more enormous it seemed.

Mark had an arm looped around Tilly's neck and was practically embracing her.

A faint memory from Sophie's childhood tugged at her—a memory of her grandfather coaxing her to hold a baby hedgehog. She'd been frightened of the prickly quills, but, once Granddad had shown her how to hold the spiny little ball, she'd been totally charmed by its soft underbelly and the little purring sound it had made.

And meeting the dogs just now had been a breeze.

'What the heck?' Sophie's heart pounded and her hand shook as she reached up. She tried not to look at those huge horsy teeth. 'He-hello, Tilly.' Very quickly she patted the short hair on Tilly's nose, then snatched her hand away.

Done. And her fingers had survived. Phew. Not so bad after all.

'Which horse do you mostly ride?' she asked hastily, hoping that her question might serve to divert attention from her nervousness.

'Charcoal.' Mark pointed to the black horse.

Of course, Mark *would* ride the biggest and scariest horse of all.

'Have you ever fallen off?'

He grinned at her. 'Tons of times.'

Sophie winced. 'Have you been badly hurt?'

'Broken leg. Concussion. Torn ligaments in my shoulder.'

The very thought of his injuries made her blanch. 'How old were you when you learned to ride?'

'I can't remember.' Mark smiled and shook his head. 'It seems like I've been on a horse all my life.' Suddenly he was climbing the railings. 'Charcoal and I are old mates.'

Sophie started to protest that a demonstration wasn't necessary, but Mark had already reached the top rail. For a heart-stopping moment, he was poised on the thin slat of timber, then, in one swift, athletic leap, he was on Charcoal's back.

She gave a shriek of alarm. He had no saddle or reins. How on earth would he stay on? Her heart was in her mouth as she watched him nudge Charcoal with his knees, saw the huge black beast lift its head in a snort then take off, its hooves thundering across the hard ground, with Mark astride him.

'Be careful!' she called, her heart thudding as fast as the horse's hooves. But her words weren't heeded.

And she soon saw that they weren't necessary. By the time Charcoal had cantered to the far end of the field, she could see that Mark and the animal moved as one—both lean and muscular, superbly athletic. Magnificent creatures, perfectly attuned to each other, and in the prime of condition and fitness.

Near the line of trees that bordered the creek, Charcoal turned in a wide arc, then came racing back at breakneck speed, Mark leaning forward, head down and holding the horse's mane. And as they drew near Mark grinned broadly at Sophie, then sat upright and threw both arms triumphantly above his head, like an Olympian acknowledging the roar of the crowd.

'Crazy idiot,' she muttered, but she was smiling. She couldn't deny he was rather splendid. And incredibly sexy. She felt a burst of feminine longing so fierce she cried out. And was glad that he couldn't hear it.

As they walked back to the house, it occurred to her that she was gradually losing her fear of the Outback, which boded well for future visits. But she was caught in a new dilemma.

It was all very fine for her to feel more at home on Coolabah Waters, but wasn't it foolish to let herself fall in love with its gorgeous owner?

CHAPTER EIGHT

MARK'S neighbours, Sophie discovered next day, lived in a large homestead, not unlike the one on Coolabah Waters—low-set, with timber walls and an iron roof, and deep, shady verandas. But the difference was that their house was surrounded by lots of shade trees and, to Sophie's surprise, green lawns.

It was painted pristine-white, with a dark green roof. Green trims on the window sills and veranda railings made it look cool and thoroughly inviting.

Andrew and Jill Jackson were tall, slim and fair, in their late thirties, with wide, welcoming smiles that gave an impression of salt-of-the-earth wholesomeness. There were three children—two long-legged girls and a little boy of six, who was a pint-sized version of his father.

'The children love visitors,' Jill said with a laugh as she led Sophie and Mark to a grouping of cane chairs on a shaded veranda. 'You're a great excuse for them to get out of schoolwork.'

'Where do you go to school?' Sophie asked them.

'In our schoolroom here at home,' said the eldest, Katie.

'Long-distance education,' Jill explained as she poured frosty glasses of home-made ginger beer. 'Their lessons are sent out by mail, and they each have thirty minutes on the phone every day with their teacher in Mount Isa. Some properties have governesses, but I'm home tutor for my three, and I really enjoy it.'

Sophie tried to imagine being tutored by her mother. *Impossible.* Lady Eliza had always been far too busy.

She was surprised that the children were encouraged to join in the conversation, and she listened while they chatted about their recent holiday on Magnetic Island.

Andrew asked Mark about the muster, and the men talked about a computer program that would allow them to monitor the condition of their paddocks via satellite photography. This interested Sophie immensely, but she kept quiet. She didn't want to give the impression that she was any more than an overseas visitor.

But when she went to the kitchen with Jill, to help carry salads to the table for lunch, she couldn't help asking, 'Were the children born out here?'

'Heavens, no,' Jill said, shaking her head. 'I went into Mount Isa Hospital.'

'But that's a long way to travel when you're in labour.'

'Oh, I wasn't in labour,' Jill assured her, as she drizzled vinaigrette onto rocket leaves. 'Pregnant women out here have to go into town when they reach thirty-six weeks. It's a requirement—to be on the safe side.'

'Oh, I see. That's sensible, I guess, but it's a bit of a nuisance, isn't it?'

Jill shrugged. 'It's just another thing you get used to when you live in the bush.'

'What about during your pregnancy? How did you manage doctor's visits?'

'A doctor comes out to Wandabilla from Mount Isa

every week to conduct a clinic. He brings his ultrasound machine, so it isn't too much of a drama.' Jill sent her a sharply curious glance and waited, almost as if she was expecting Sophie to explain her interest in Outback pregnancy.

But although this woman seemed very nice Sophie wasn't ready to confide. Instead, she asked, 'Have you always lived out here?'

Jill shook her head. 'I grew up in the city. In Adelaide, in the south. I trained to be a nurse with Andrew's sister, and I went home with her once for a holiday, set eyes on Andrew and…' She grinned. 'And that same afternoon I helped him to vaccinate a pen of steers. Wouldn't let the poor man out of my sight.' She winked. 'But he didn't seem to mind.'

Sophie wanted to ask if she had any regrets about leaving the city, but Jill was looking at her shrewdly again, as if she had questions of her own to ask. Luckily, Anna burst into the kitchen to announce that young John had already begun to help himself to the potato salad, so the questions were dropped.

Sophie enjoyed the lunch very much. Corned beef, she discovered, was very tasty, especially when accompanied by home-made mango chutney. They ate in a large dining room, not unlike Mark's, but painted in a cool lemon and white, with pretty curtains framing a view of the lush and shady garden. When Sophie admired the garden, Jill offered her cuttings.

'Well…thank you,' Sophie said awkwardly.

'Sophie's only going to be here for another week or so,' Mark intervened. 'And that's hardly long enough to get a garden established, is it?'

This was met by puzzled silence. Across the table Jill's gaze met her husband's.

And Sophie's eyes met Mark's, but his expression was distinctly guarded.

Jill broke the awkward silence. 'Leave the plants till you come back, then, Sophie. In the meantime I'll pot up a few things for you. To get you started.'

Now it was Sophie's turn to feel confused. She wasn't coming back. What had Mark told the Jacksons about her? She shot him another searching glance, but he kept his eyes on his plate, as if those last slices of cucumber and carrot were the most important vegetables in the world.

If Jill noticed the tension, she didn't let on. 'Time for dessert,' she said. 'Who has room for lemon-chiffon pie?'

This time, when Sophie glanced Mark's way, she caught a small smile twitching the corners of his mouth. 'I'd love some, thanks,' he said, sending Sophie a slow wink that made her toes curl. 'Lemon-chiffon is my favourite.'

An embarassing heat warmed Sophie's face as she re-membered what had happened the last time they'd eaten this dessert. In London after the wedding.

'Let me help you, Jill,' she said, jumping to her feet.

It was when everyone was tucking into their pie that Jill said, 'Mark's told us about your famous musical family, Sophie.'

Andrew chimed in. 'My grandfather was very musi-cal, and we still have his grand piano, but it never gets used now. No one else in the family has ever shown any interest.'

'Except me,' piped up Anna, and then she pouted. 'But I can't have piano lessons until I go to boarding school.'

Sophie sent her a sympathetic smile.

'I'm sure you can play, can't you, Sophie?' prompted Jill. 'Maybe you could give Anna a few tips?'

Sophie was so used to denying any musical ability that she almost said no. She had too many painful memories of dire occasions in her childhood when she'd been forced to play for her parents' guests and had suffered the embarrassment of comparison with her brilliant sisters.

But this was a very different scene.

'I can play a little,' she admitted.

Anna clapped her hands. 'Will you play for us now?'

'Please do,' added Jill. 'It's an age since our piano was played properly, but I get it tuned every year just the same.'

'It would be a pleasant change to hear proper music and not the kids' tuneless thumping,' chimed in Andrew.

Everyone looked expectantly at Sophie.

'I don't have any music,' she said.

This was met by a chorus of groans.

And when Sophie saw Anna's crestfallen face she gave in. 'I can play simple things by ear,' she amended, but she didn't admit that she actually preferred playing by ear, improvising as the mood took her.

'Wonderful.' Jill leapt to her feet. 'The piano's in the lounge. Everyone go in there and I'll bring the coffee.'

It was three in the afternoon before Sophie and Mark reluctantly agreed that they should make their departure.

'You were a great hit,' Mark said as they drove back across the flat, sparsely treed plains, heading for Coolabah Waters. He shot Sophie a questioning glance. 'I thought you said you weren't musical.'

'Compared to the rest of the family, I'm not.'

'But you're fabulous. I bet your sisters can't play all those movie themes and pop songs by ear.'

'Well, no. I don't think they know many pop songs.'

'There you go,' he cried, giving the steering wheel a delighted thump. 'We don't need concert-standard performances at an old-fashioned Outback singalong.'

She smiled. 'It was fun, wasn't it?'

'It was terrific. The Jacksons loved you. I was very proud of you.' Mark looked suddenly embarrassed, as if he'd said too much.

But his praise sent a giddy thrill swirling through Sophie. 'Young Anna is very talented. She has an exceptional ear for a child. I felt bad when I had to explain that I wouldn't be able to teach her, that I'm going back to England.' She frowned at Mark. 'I don't understand why they think I'm staying on.'

His only reply was a throat-clearing sound and Sophie turned square on to him, crossing her arms over her chest. 'Is this confession time, Mark?'

'What are you talking about?' He flicked a quick look her way then speedily returned to staring at the track ahead.

'As if you don't know.' Sophie rolled her eyes even though he wasn't looking at her. 'Why do your neighbours think I'm here to stay?'

His jaw jutted stubbornly. 'They've just made an assumption.'

'Andrew and Jill don't strike me as the types who jump to conclusions on very little evidence. What did you tell them?'

'I simply told them you were a girl I met in England.'

'But they knew about my family. What else did you tell them?'

His shoulders lifted in an uneasy shrug. 'Not much at all. But word spreads quickly in the bush. And when your phone call came through on that mustering camp it caused quite a stir.'

'Really?' Sophie was faintly appalled. 'Why?'

'Well…it's not every day a man, out in the middle of a bush muster, gets a phone call from a girl in England.'

She frowned. 'Don't tell me all the men were listening in?'

'They weren't eavesdropping. They couldn't hear our conversation. But they knew you were calling from England, and they knew I'd been over there for the wedding. And now you've turned up here. I guess everyone has put two and two together.'

'And they've come up with five.'

After a beat, Mark said, 'When it should have been three.'

Sophie stared at him and gulped.

Three… The two of them plus their baby…

Unexpected sadness stung her throat, and she turned away and watched a mob of cattle moving quietly across the flat expanse of a golden paddock. She remembered how distraught she'd been when she'd rung Mark from London, thought now about how embarrassed he must have been when he'd had to take her surprising call in front of a bunch of stockmen.

Now Mark's friends and neighbours had visions of a romance between them. They probably expected him to marry her.

If there was no wedding and she went back to

England, they were going to be jolly disappointed for Mark. No doubt the gossip would start again, and Mark would be left with the awkward job of trying to shrug off her reasons for abandoning him.

And in England, she would be facing equally awkward questions from her parents. *Ouch.*

What a mess.

Sophie sagged against the car door and stared at the blur of pale-gold paddocks outside.

At the Jackson's today, she'd begun to sense that life in the Outback could be quite wonderful for a woman and a man who loved each other. The isolation of the bush demanded something special of a couple. Away from the hustle and bustle of city life, people focused on caring for each other and their children. She'd never met such a close-knit, happy family.

There had actually been a heady moment when Sophie had thought that perhaps she could live here and be a successful Outback wife, too. Jill was a wonderful inspiration—contented with her busy life, running the house as well as supervising her children's schooling and helping her husband with the business side of running their cattle property.

Sophie had begun to imagine living that kind of life with Mark. And during the fun of the singalong her eyes had caught Mark's and she'd seen such warmth and happiness in his face that she'd thought that perhaps marriage with him was more than possible.

But face it, she thought now as they sped over the dirt track, there were major differences between her and Jill Jackson.

For heaven's sake, on the very first afternoon Jill had

arrived in the Outback she'd helped Andrew to vaccinate a pen of steers. For Sophie, the very thought of doing anything like that was laughable. But, beyond that, Jill and Andrew were a perfect love-match.

Love. That was the catch.

A pang settled around Sophie's heart. She doubted that Mark loved her. Oh, he was being very kind and patient with her, but she could never be the sort of girl he would really want to share his life with. He needed a very different breed of woman as his Outback wife.

No way could Sophie jump into a pen of steers. She was too frightened to give a horse's nose a decent pat, let alone climb aboard and ride one. She wore silly sandals with daisies instead of sensible elastic-sided boots. She could make fancy desserts, but she hadn't a clue how to cook corned beef.

Mark was all too aware of this. He knew she had little potential as a cattleman's wife.

And, unfortunately, there wasn't much she could do to change his mind.

Or was there?

At dinner that evening, Sophie paused with her fork midway between her plate and her mouth and asked, 'What happens when you go out mustering, Mark? Where do you sleep?'

Mark almost choked. Questions from Sophie about his sleeping habits had a bad effect on his table manners. She was looking incredibly lovely this evening. A flush of pink tinted her cheeks and pretty lights danced in her eyes. And she was wearing slim-fitting white jeans and a camisole top of pale-lavender silk with a fetching lace trim that skimmed the tops of her breasts.

And she wanted to talk about beds! *Have mercy, woman!*

'We sleep in a swag,' he told her quickly.

'In a *what*?' Her big grey eyes widened, looked lost.

'A swag. It's a lightweight mattress that rolls up inside waterproof canvas.'

'But you put these swags inside tents, don't you?'

Smiling at her worried frown, he shook his head. 'We sleep out in the open, under the stars.'

'Really?' Her eyes, if possible, grew wider. 'With nothing to protect you?'

'Tents are cumbersome.' He was struggling to concentrate on her questions and not on the thought of sleeping with her—in a swag, in a tent—her sweet curves snuggled close…

Whoa, boy! Heel.

Mark dragged in a hasty breath. 'Tents are too much trouble,' he said. 'We muster in the dry season, so there's hardly ever any rain. And you can always hang a tarpaulin between a couple of trees if it gets a bit wet.'

'So you just lie on—on the *ground*, out in the open?'

'Sure. But the swags are surprisingly comfortable. And there's nothing better than sleeping under the stars.'

Sophie looked worried, took a sip from her water glass. 'Do women like Jill Jackson sleep in swags, too?'

'Absolutely.' And then, because he couldn't help himself, Mark gave her a slow, teasing smile. 'You'd love it out there, curled in a swag and listening to the sounds of the bush at night.'

She looked paler than ever.

'So why don't we try it one night?'

What in the name of fortune had made him say that? No way would Sophie say yes.

She smiled shyly. 'I'd love to give it a go.'

Sophie stared up at the stars through the fine mosquito net suspended above her swag. She could hardly believe she was doing this. She was terrified and thrilled at once.

She told herself she was perfectly safe. Mark slept out in the open like this all the time. And, after all, they were only lying on the top of the creek bank, a few hundred metres from the house. Mark had kindly insisted that she must go back inside if it all got too much.

But, to her surprise, she discovered that he was right about the swag. It was actually quite comfy. She was safely cocooned in a flannelette-lined sleeping bag wrapped in canvas. There was a slim but adequate mattress beneath her, and the mosquito net to protect her from nasty creepy-crawlies, so there really wasn't anything to complain about.

And once she'd stopped fretting about the complete lack of electric lighting, and the fact that there were no walls around her, no roof above and no floor below, she was fine. If she could stop obsessing about Mark lying so close, she would really be able to appreciate this gorgeous evening.

The night air was cool and sweet, and the sky was crystal clear and studded with diamond-bright stars.

Actually, the sky was truly amazing…an astonishing dome arching over them.

Huge. Spectacular.

A miracle.

As for the moon! The quarter moon lay against the black velvet of the sky like a curled piece of hammered silver suspended within a faint circle, the promise of the full moon to come.

It reminded Sophie of her baby in her womb. Admittedly, it didn't take much to make her think about that these days. She slipped her hand under the waistband of her tracksuit, let it lie protectively over her tummy. Wondered about the little person she nurtured there.

One day in the future her child would come to visit Mark at Coolabah Waters. And he would bring the child out here at night to show off these glorious stars. This moon.

The two of them would be together here. And where would she be? Back in England, waiting jealously for her child's return? She blinked, and her vision grew misty as she turned to Mark's large, dark shape lying beside her in his separate swag.

As if he'd sensed her movement, he turned, too, and his deep, rumbly voice came out of the darkness. 'Everything OK?'

'Yes, thanks. Absolutely fine,' she said. She was glad of the darkness as she used a corner of the flannelette sheet to wipe her eye. 'But I'm sure I'll never actually get to sleep. I don't want to stop looking at the sky. It's so amazing. I knew there were lots of stars, but I had no idea there were as many as this.'

Mark chuckled softly. 'There are about two billion in the Milky Way alone. And what we see here is only the tip of the iceberg as far as the universe is concerned.'

'It takes my breath away. The stars are so bright! So beautiful.'

'That's because there's no artificial light out here, no glare from cities or towns to diminish the starlight.'

She remembered him looking for the stars in London and being disappointed.

Now they both lay very still, staring above at the sky, and listening to the occasional sounds that broke the silence—the spooky call of a bird that Mark called a mopoke, a low bellow from a distant cow, and the hoot of an owl that kept vigil over the starlit paddocks from a branch in a tree further down the creek.

'Do you know the names of any of those stars?' she asked.

'A few.'

'Which ones?'

'Well, the most famous constellation Down Under is the Southern Cross. Over there to the south you can see two bright stars in a vertical line above the horizon—they're the pointers—and if you follow them up you'll come to the cross. Four good-sized stars and a tiny one.'

'Yes, I see them.'

'Can you see the saucepan shape straight up above us?'

'Yes.'

'That's Orion. The handle of the saucepan is the hilt of his sword. And the V up there on the right?'

'Yup. Got it.'

'They're the horns of Taurus the bull.'

She laughed. 'Taurus is my star sign.'

As she stared at it, a streak of light seemed to come out of nowhere and shoot across the sky.

'Look!' she cried, making a dint in the mosquito net as she sat up quickly. 'Is that a falling star?'

The burning arc of fire zoomed downwards, heading for the horizon, and leaving a golden trail of sparks behind it like a skyrocket.

'We see a lot of them out here,' Mark said casually.

A lot of falling stars? How amazing! Sophie had been sure it was a once-in-a-lifetime experience.

'And there's a satellite,' he said, pointing.

'Where?'

'Directly above that tall ironbark tree. See it moving?'

Sophie caught it—a tiny, tiny light travelling bravely through the vast sea of stars.

Wow! She'd had no idea the night sky could be so absorbing. She lay down again, staring all about her, and felt again a strange sense of connection, just as she had on the day they'd gone fencing—an unexpected but deep connection with planet Earth, with the sky above and the ground beneath her, the creatures out there in the bush—the entire universe.

I feel different, she thought. *Out here I feel different about everything.*

Her life in London, her job, her friends and family, seemed so remote. She knew they were only a phone call or a plane trip away, but they belonged to another world, a world that seemed less real than this. Concerts and cafés, city buildings and crowds couldn't really compare with this simple, natural spectacle.

I can be myself here.

She could *find* herself here, find the real Sophie—not someone trying to pretend, forever trying to live up to the expectations of others.

Except, she thought with a heavy sigh, if she stayed here she would soon become just as busy trying to turn herself into the kind of woman that Mark needed, a perfect woman of the Outback.

'A penny for your thoughts.'

Mark's voice startled her.

In the darkness, Sophie blushed. 'I—I was wondering if anyone in my family has ever seen stars like this,' she said.

'Do you miss your family?'

'Not a lot,' she answered honestly. 'They're so busy, I hardly see them anyhow. I'm sure they're not missing me.' After a small silence, she asked shyly, 'What about you, Mark? What were you thinking about?'

At first he didn't answer, and then he released a long, heavy breath. 'I'm trying to come to terms with the fact that my child isn't going to see these stars at night, or hear the sounds of the bush.'

Sophie's throat tightened. 'Does that worry you?'

'To be honest, I hate the thought of him or her growing up without knowing the call of the curlews, or a kookaburra's laugh, even the howl of a distant dingo. It might sound strange to you, but these things give me comfort. I guess they're in my blood.'

The tightness in her throat became painful. 'But the baby, she or he, will…will come to visit you.'

There was no response.

She turned to him, felt her heart tumble when she saw his grim profile silvered by moonlight. She wanted to tell him that she could stay. She didn't have to go back to England. But surely it was his role to invite her?

She swallowed to relieve the ache in her throat. 'Mark, I promise I'll make it as easy as I can for you to have access.'

He grunted. 'That's all very easy to say.'

'I mean it.' She wished he were looking at her, wished he could see her face, wanted him to see her sincerity.

'I know you mean it now,' he said. 'But have you really thought ahead, Sophie? What about when you get married?'

'*Married?*' Her startled cry was close to a shriek.

'Don't sound so surprised. You know it's going to happen.'

But she didn't know anything of the sort. If Mark was talking about her marrying someone else, right now that seemed an impossible thought.

'You're a fabulous woman,' he went on. 'You're not going to be a single mum for the rest of your life. In weeks, months, maybe even years down the track, you're going to meet the man of your dreams. And how do you think your child's biological father will fit into the scheme of things then?'

'You'll…' The words died on Sophie's lips. She had no idea. Until tonight, she hadn't let herself think much further than telling her family about the baby.

She tried to see herself in the future Mark predicted—married to an Englishman, living in London—tried to imagine how a strange man would feel about taking Mark's child into his home. There was every chance he would be quite fine about it. Blended families were practically the norm these days.

Meanwhile, Mark would be back here in Australia, alone in the big, empty house, wishing he could be with his child. A glacial chill crept down her spine.

Mark had so much to offer as a father. He was a successful and confident man, at ease with himself and his surroundings, as steady as a rock, and interesting, too—a deep and passionate man with a vision for the future. And for him that future should include the raising of his child.

And... She really, really liked him.

She'd never met anyone like him before, and she'd never experienced anything remotely *close* to the wonderful night they'd spent together in London. She might never experience it again.

Again, she tried to picture herself back in England—happy, independent and getting on with her life—but the picture wouldn't hold, kept disintegrating before her eyes. Panic gripped her.

She'd stepped out on a limb by coming to Australia, but she'd felt safe, because she'd known she could always go back to England. Her family would be upset, it would be horrible for a bit, but then they'd settle down and adjust.

But now she felt as if that limb she'd stepped onto was beginning to crack under the weight of uncertainty. Going back to London felt much less appealing than staying here with Mark.

It would help if Mark loved her, if he hadn't merely let her stay because they had a baby's future to sort out.

For a fraught moment, Sophie had a terrible sense of not belonging *anywhere*. A deep loneliness took hold, wrapping its fingers around her throat, squeezing a miserable sob from her.

She heard a rustling sound in the swag beside her.

'Sophie, are you OK?'

'No.'

Mark sat up. 'Have you had enough of it out here? Would you like to go back inside?'

'No.' It was little more than a bleat, but quite definite.

He stared into the shadows where she lay. She could see his face, caught in the starlight, and he looked like something a master craftsman would sculpt in marble, all strong, masculine planes and angles.

'Is there anything you'd like?' he asked her.

'Yes.' Suddenly certain, she sat up, her heart thudding, her limbs trembling. 'I'd like you to hold me, Mark.'

There was an embarrassingly long stretch of silence during which the owl hooted again.

'You do realise what you're saying?' he said at last. 'Remember, you insisted I keep my dist—'

'I know,' Sophie interjected quickly, and she shoved the mosquito net roughly aside. 'It's OK, Mark.'

Mark tensed all over, was seized by a shuddering jolt of desire. *Oh, God.* He was aching with his need for this woman. The temptation she presented was agonising. He'd been crazy to think he could spend a night sleeping next to Sophie without needing to hold her.

But Sophie had known the danger of attachment when she'd first arrived here, and she was right—if they spent a night together, if they made love again, they would only make their problems worse. Parting again, sending her back to England where she belonged, would be so much harder.

Why couldn't she stick to her own damn rules?

'But you insisted that we mustn't,' he groaned. 'You made me promise.'

'I've changed my mind.'

Mark heard a choked cry, was aware of Sophie hurling herself across the short, dark chasm of night that separated them. Next moment his arms were full of her. Sweet smelling, sexy Sophie.

His heart thundered. All he wanted was to crush her to him, to taste her sweetness, kiss her senseless, to fling her down on his mattress and cover her with kisses from head to toe, to lose himself in her, to experience again that wild, wonderful, electrifying passion they'd shared in London.

Why was she tempting him?

Couldn't she remember that this was wrong? There were a thousand reasons. She'd been so very certain that she didn't want any physical intimacy with him. She'd made that mistake once, and she was paying the highest price.

He held her carefully in his lap, as if she were fragile and might break into a thousand pieces, and tried to ignore the clamouring need rampaging through him. Against her ear, he whispered, 'Aren't you worried that this will complicate everything?'

She shook her head, and her silky hair brushed his cheek, eliciting a soft moan from him.

'Not any more, Mark.' Her voice was a sensuous, breathy whisper. 'I've realised now that this *simplifies* everything.'

She turned in his arms, and her soft, trembling lips brushed his jaw. Her subtle perfume surrounded him, and he felt the soft pressure of her lush, round breasts against his chest.

Mark knew he was a drowning man. How could he *not* kiss her?

And then, heaven help him, her arms twined around his neck. Her eager lips parted, and he dipped his mouth to taste her. Their tongues touched, tentatively at first, and then with familiar delight and building need.

At last.

At last.

Sweet shivers rippled over Sophie's skin, and her insides melted and tumbled as Mark clasped the sides of her head, as his fingers plunged roughly into her hair, and he showered her with kisses—over her face, over her throat, and into the dip of her collarbone.

He buried his face against her shoulder. 'You sweet thing,' he uttered between ragged breaths. 'Do you have any idea how wild you make me?'

'It's the same for me,' she whispered, pressing kisses to the hectic pulse in his neck.

She traced trembling fingers down the line of his jaw and he caught her fingers, kissed and nibbled them, sending rivers of pleasure coursing through her. Then, with a soft groan, his lips found hers again and he took her mouth urgently, deeply, with a forceful possession that thrilled her.

His hands slipped beneath her T-shirt and found her breasts. He stroked her gently, spreading wonderful heat spiralling outwards and downwards. His fingers squeezed, and she flinched momentarily.

He pulled his hand away. 'Sorry. Are you tender?'

'Just a little.'

'I don't want to hurt you.' He removed his hand completely, but Sophie clasped it in hers, took it shyly, impatiently, and pressed it against her.

'Don't worry, Mark.'

'I can be slow and gentle,' he breathed, tucking her

head against his shoulder, and tracing feathery, soft circles over her with his fingertips.

'Yes,' she whispered. 'I remember. You have wonderfully slow hands.'

'I remember everything about making love to you, Sophie. Every touch, every kiss, is imprinted on me for all time.'

Gathering her close, he guided her gently backwards until she was lying on his mattress.

In a breathless daze, she looked up at him. 'Will there be enough room in one swag for both of us?'

A brief grin slashed the dark intensity in his face. 'I believe we'll manage.'

She reached up to him. He lowered his long body beside her and they were together at last.

Together. In the darkness, with only the stars as their witness, they shared achingly sweet kisses and heated caresses. Together they sought the intimacy they craved, confessed the need they'd not dared acknowledge with words.

CHAPTER NINE

SOPHIE hoped that the words might come afterwards when they lay wrapped in each other's arms, watching the glittering sky. But Mark was strangely silent.

He held her close, almost possessively, but he stared above at the stars as if he was lost in thought.

She snuggled into him, pressed a kiss into the musky shadows on his neck. 'Thank you,' she whispered.

'Thank *you*,' he said softly, and his arm tightened around her shoulders.

She waited for him to say something more, something about his feelings for her, wondered if she should lead the way. Should she tell him she'd never met a man who made her feel so happy, so appreciated and sexy?

His silence and the fact that she'd initiated this whole event stilled her tongue. She'd practically begged him to make love to her; she wasn't going to beg him for compliments afterwards.

And she wasn't going to get into a stew about his silence. She knew guys found it difficult to talk about their feelings, and she'd read in a magazine that they hated post-mortems about dates or parties or sex.

Especially sex. She would have to be patient. All would be revealed in the morning.

With no curtains or roof to hold back the daylight, Sophie woke at dawn for almost the first time in her life.

She lay with her head against the strong wall of Mark's chest and watched in a kind of hushed awe as the sun pushed ruddy fingers above the trees. Soon blue, red and gold streaks appeared in the clouds. The dawn was truly beautiful, more beautiful than any holiday sunset.

As the brilliance faded, light spread across the sky like a stain remover, sapping the heavens of darkness and casting a creamy warmth over the quiet, misty bush.

Sophie thought about the stars that had been so brilliant last night. They were still up there somewhere, invisible now.

She closed her eyes, overpowered by the memories of last night. She wondered if the amazing tenderness and intimacy she and Mark had shared would, like the stars, disappear with the arrival of the sun.

Turning, she looked at Mark. Feasted her eyes on him. From this angle she could see the underside of his jaw, the strong bones beneath his skin and the first signs of his beard's regrowth.

She pressed a wake-up kiss to his shoulder and he stirred, rolling sideways. He opened his eyes and smiled, and released a playful growl as he reached for her.

'I knew I was going to love waking up next to you.' He pressed his lips to the side of her brow. 'How are you this morning?'

'Wonderful.'

'No upset tummy?'

'No,' she said, surprised. *Fancy that*. She hadn't even thought about morning sickness. Perhaps it was over already.

Wriggling closer, she slipped an arm around his neck and nibbled his ear. 'If we were out on a muster, what would happen now?'

Mark chuckled. 'If we were on a muster, we'd have been up and gone from here long ago.'

'I'm glad we're not on a muster, then.'

'So am I,' he murmured, giving her neck a sleepy nuzzle.

'I could stay here all day.'

'No you couldn't.' He kissed her chin.

Sophie was certain she could camp right here in this swag with Mark for the rest of her life. 'Could, too,' she said smugly.

'No way.' He trailed his lips over hers. 'The sun would send you inside before eight o'clock.'

She sighed. 'I forgot about the sun.'

With the softest touch, Mark's fingers traced the line of her backbone. 'You must never forget about the sun in the Outback.' He looked at her through half-closed lashes. 'That's why we have a rule out here.' Cupping her bottom, he gathered her into him. 'You should never waste time in the morning.'

'That sounds like—' Sophie began, but Mark's lips cut her off in mid-sentence.

She didn't mind in the least. This was *exactly* what she wanted.

* * *

The sun had climbed quite high by the time they drove the ute the short distance back to the homestead. As Mark parked it beneath the mango tree and slipped the keys from the ignition, he turned to Sophie, and the light shining in his eyes made her heart leap high.

'Why don't you stay?' he said.

'Stay?' she repeated. There was nothing she wanted more than to stay here with this gorgeous, gorgeous man, but she was scared that she might misinterpret his meaning.

'Stay longer than two weeks.' He smiled, and the skin around his eyes crinkled. 'We seem to like each other, don't we?'

'Seems so,' she said breathlessly.

His slow smile climbed his cheeks. 'Is that a yes? You'll stay?'

Oh, man. Sophie couldn't breathe, she was so excited and scared. 'How—how long were you thinking?' *A month, three?* 'I'd have to arrange for someone to take care of my business. And there's a cut-off point when the airlines won't take pregnant women.'

'If you can sort out your business, couldn't you have the baby here?'

Her heart took off like a skyrocket.

Watching her, Mark's smile faded. 'Is that a bad idea, Sophie?'

She shook her head. 'No, it's not a bad idea.'

'Would you be worried about having the baby out here?'

'No. I've talked to Jill, and she told me about the doctors and hospitals and everything. It seems to be perfectly safe to be pregnant in the Outback.'

Mark reached for her hands. 'I'll take care of you. We can fix up the house, choose somewhere to make a nursery.'

'Are you sure, Mark?'

His throat worked, and he looked down at their linked hands. 'I know we're still getting to know each other better. I'm not asking you to commit to anything permanent.' He lifted his gaze and smiled nervously. 'Down the track, if you realise that it's not going to work out, you should feel completely free to head back to England.'

Sophie gulped. It made perfect sense that Mark should offer her a way out if their relationship didn't work. He was being perfectly logical and reasonable, perfectly *perfect* actually.

So why was she feeling nervous?

Why couldn't she have more faith in herself? It was such a bore to be afraid of failure.

'Don't look like that, Sophie. What's the matter?'

Mark was frowning at her.

Her hands lifted in a gesture of helplessness. 'I'm just being a goose. Finding things to worry about that aren't really problems.'

'Are you worried about ringing your parents? Would you like me to speak to them?

'No, no. It's OK. I'll ring home tonight.'

To her surprise, having said that, she felt immediately better.

Sophie rang home before dinner that evening, and she was immensely relieved that it was her mother who answered.

'I just wanted to let you know there's been a slight change of plans,' she said, getting straight to the point with deceptive confidence. 'I've decided to stay on here.'

'How…nice,' her mother replied carefully. 'I assume that means you're staying on at Coolabah Waters with Mark?'

'Yes.' Sophie's heart began an anxious hammering. 'We…want more time to get to know each other better.'

'So you really like this young man, darling?'

'Yes,' Sophie said, wishing she didn't feel so nervous about the other news she had to deliver.

Her mother's voice sounded so close, as if she was in the same room, and Sophie wished she could see her face. Right now she could do with a motherly hug to smooth the way for this difficult conversation. Lady Eliza's busy life as an operatic diva hadn't spared much time for nurturing a close and easy intimacy with her youngest, most mystifying daughter.

Sophie's grandfather had filled the role of confidant, but even he hadn't been much help when it had come to boyfriends. They'd been Emma's territory.

Sophie took a deep breath. 'There's something else I should tell you, Mum.'

'Yes, dear?'

Instinctively she closed her eyes, and her face screwed up tightly as she dropped her bombshell. 'You're going to be a grandmother.'

'Good heavens!'

Silence followed.

Sophie felt sick. 'It happened in England, Mum. That's why I came down here, to see Mark. We're trying to sort things out.'

'You mean your wedding plans?'

'Well, no. We—we don't want to rush into marriage.' Sophie was so glad Mark wasn't listening.

'But you are planning to be married?'

'Nothing definite at this stage.'

There was an anguished sigh on the other end of the line.

Sophie chewed her lip. *The family failure strikes again!*

'Mum, don't worry about me. I'm fine.'

'Are you sure, dear? Are you keeping well?'

'Fit as the proverbial fiddle.'

'And—and Mark's taking good care of you?'

'He's being very sweet.'

'If I wasn't so busy, I'd come and visit you.'

'Oh, there's no need. Honestly.' Sophie blanched at the thought of Lady Eliza arriving in Wandabilla. Her mother would take one look at the place and want to cart Sophie back to London pronto.

'Mum, would you mind breaking the news gently to Dad? It might be better coming from you.'

'Of course, dear. It's always a matter of timing with your father. I'll wait for the right moment, and handle it so beautifully he'll slip into grandfather mode without realising it.'

'Thanks. You're a star.'

'You are happy, aren't you, Sophie? About the baby?'

'Oh, yes, I'm rapt,' she said. 'Don't worry, Mum, I really am excited. And Mark's excited, too.'

There was a distinct sigh of relief. 'Good. When all's said and done, if you're both happy nothing else matters, does it?'

'No,' said Sophie softly.

Fingers crossed, it really was as simple as that.

Telling her mum had certainly been a lot easier than she'd expected. And to think she'd been so stressed!

There's been a real turnaround in my life.

No doubt about it—after last night's love-making under the stars, and Marks' wonderful invitation to stay, she felt like a brand-new woman.

Flowers—where had they come from?

Mark stared at the kitchen table. They were eating in there tonight, had agreed it was cosier.

And it looked especially cosy with a simple jam-jar filled with deep red, purple and yellow flowers. There was no doubt the splashes of colour brightened the room. He looked more closely at the centrepiece and saw that the red flower was a rose.

A rose? Out here?

Sophie came from the stove, carrying a casserole dish wrapped in an oven cloth.

'Are these flowers real?' he asked her.

She laughed as she set the dish carefully down on a cane mat. 'Of course. Smell the rose. It's gorgeous.'

Mark dipped his nose low, and caught a sweet, almost forgotten perfume that took him straight back to his childhood. 'But how did it get here?' He gave the rose another sniff. 'It hasn't come all the way from England, has it?'

This roused another laugh, plus a jaunty toss of Sophie's glossy dark curls and a flash of pearly teeth. Mark felt at that moment that he could watch her for ever.

She lifted the lid of a casserole dish. 'I found the rose in *your* garden, Mark.'

With a shake of his head, he grinned. 'I didn't even know I had a garden.'

'Well, no self-respecting gardener would claim ownership.' She paused in the process of spooning rice onto their plates and smiled reproachfully. 'There are only a few poor straggling plants that aren't weeds.'

As they took their places, she said, 'I don't know how Jill Jackson managed to get such a lovely garden growing at Blue Hills.'

'You'd be surprised. Thanks to bore water, lots of homesteads have lovely gardens. My mother always had a fabulous garden at Wynstead.'

Just talking about his mother's garden brought back memories of his childhood. He and his sister had played endlessly, running over the long sweep of smooth, green lawn, climbing the enormous tamarind tree. Countless hours they'd spent, playing hide and seek beneath the huge, leafy hibiscus bushes, catching tadpoles in the fern-fringed lily pond.

And in his mother's house there'd always been flowers on the hall table, on the sideboard, on coffee tables and on the dining table, always lots of colour to please the eye and to make the house welcoming.

Just like this arrangement, he thought, staring at Sophie's flowers.

As they ate, Mark cast a critical eye over his kitchen. He knew it was drab, but now he tried to see it as an outsider might. No doubt about it, his house was in need of a paint job. The dining room and bedrooms were even worse than the kitchen. And women cared about things like that.

'My mother kept the inside of the house lovely, too,'

he admitted. 'Lots of paintings and knick-knacks. Beautiful furniture. She'd be horrified if she could see the way I live out here.'

'What happened to all her things when you left Wynstead?'

'Tania, my sister, took all the decorative stuff.'

'Your sister?' Sophie's eyes widened. 'You never told me you had a sister. Where does she live?'

'In Melbourne. Married to a barrister.'

'Do you see much of her?'

Mark shrugged. 'Not a lot. Those two love the city life. They're opera buffs, actually.'

Afraid that talk of the city and opera might make Sophie homesick, he hurried on. 'I need to start a few home improvements, but I could do with some advice. Do you think you could help me to shop for the things I need? We could order them online from Mount Isa.'

She favoured him with a coy smile. 'When a man mentions shopping and home improvements in the same sentence, a girl can't help being a *tad* interested.' And then she confessed, 'Actually, I'm itching to get to this place with a paint brush. I have a secret hankering to be an interior designer.'

Mark's eyebrows lifted. 'What stopped you?'

'The usual,' she said, with an offhand shrug. 'Lack of self-confidence. Fear of failure.'

He found it difficult to believe that the lovely, effervescent Sophie Felsham had problems with self-confidence. But he couldn't deny that growing up with a family of overachievers must have taken its toll.

And that Oliver fellow had done quite a number on her.

To distract her further, he said, 'Tell me how I should redecorate this place. Where should I start?'

Her grin split her face. 'You're going to regret asking that.' With almost a skip of childish glee, Sophie hurried to the kitchen dresser, grabbed a note pad and pen and darted back to her chair.

Pushing her plate to one side, she sat with her legs crossed and pen poised, and smiled at him with such anticipation that Mark wanted to kiss her.

Heaven help him.

How was he supposed to think about interior decorating when he was assailed by visions of Sophie flat on her back on the kitchen table, smiling up at him with that same breathless eagerness?

'OK,' she said, blissfully unaware of his salacious thoughts. 'Give me an idea of what you'd like, Mark.'

'A-ah…'

'What's your favourite colour?'

He was looking into her eyes. 'Grey.'

'Grey?' Sophie frowned, but dutifully made note of this.

'What rooms are most important, do you think? Where do you spend most of your time?'

'In my bedroom.'

She went pink in the cheeks. 'Are you sure? Aren't there other rooms that have priority?'

'My bedroom's the most important room in my house,' he asserted. 'I spend almost a third of my life in bed.'

With a dignified straightening of her shoulders and an arch of her right eyebrow, Sophie made another note. 'OK. Bedroom heads the list. What other parts of the house would you like to fix?'

'Come on, I'll show you.' He held out his hand to her.

'Can't you just tell me? I'm making notes here.'

'Come on, Sophie. Interior decorating is a visual art form, and you'll find it immensely helpful if you can actually see what I'm talking about.'

She rolled her eyes, letting out a huff of exaggerated annoyance as she stood. 'Oh, all right.'

Sophie had a suspicion that she knew exactly where Mark was taking her. She was dead certain when he led her down the hallway. And straight to his bedroom.

For some reason that didn't quite make sense, she felt suddenly shy as she stepped into Mark's private domain.

She'd seen this room briefly on the first day she'd arrived, when she'd been searching for a bed to collapse onto, and she knew it had a lot of potential. Without leaving the doorway, she surveyed it again.

It was actually one of those rooms that interior designers dreamed about. A room with 'good bones'— generous proportions, a high ceiling and beautiful stained-glass windows framed by a graceful archway.

But interior decorating had obviously been a very low priority for generations of previous owners. The paintwork was dark and dingy like the rest of the house. The timber floors were covered by a ghastly, grey-and-maroon floral linoleum. The window frames were peeling, putty was falling out, and the bed was a very plain double mattress on a simple wooden base made up with white sheets and an old green blanket. No duvet or quilt.

Not the slightest bit romantic.

She could well understand why Mark wanted it decorated.

He was smiling his thousand-kilowatt smile as he stood, his thumbs hooked through the belt loops on his jeans, looking about him at the walls, the ceiling and the marvellous arch.

'You don't want grey in here,' she said.

Grey was totally wrong. The house was already as drab as a wet week in London. 'This room's shaded by the big mango tree outside, so it's already cool. You want a warmer colour. But I think it should be balanced by lots of white, or maybe soft beige.'

He nodded, but the tiny smile in his eyes made her wonder if he was really listening.

'I think this room calls for something quite luscious,' she said, looking again at the gold and rose, mauve and green glass in the beautiful windows. 'What about a pale primrose on the walls combined with a really deep, lush cream for the trims? And maybe rosy accents in some of the furnishings?'

'Rosy accents?' Mark looked amused, then doubtful. 'Do you really think so?'

She nodded. 'I know it doesn't sound very masculine, but it would be stunning.' Coming into the middle of the room, she looked about her and saw the changes already in her imagination, like 'before and after' shots in a magazine.

Mark pointed to an open set of French doors. 'What do you make of this over here?'

He gestured for her to go ahead of him into a much smaller adjoining room. When she did so, she saw that it was empty apart from a large leather saddle on the floor, some old text books stacked in a corner, and a pair of rowing oars propped against one wall. But there was the sweetest circular window that looked out across the front garden.

'I guess this must have been a dressing room,' she suggested, and then she smiled as she tried to imagine Mark bothering with a dressing room to pull on jeans, a work shirt and riding boots.

Her smile faded as she was hit by another idea. 'Oh, my.'

Mark frowned. 'What?'

Her answer was little more than a whisper. 'This little room would make an absolutely darling nursery.'

She could see it already: soft carpet on the floor. A baby's white cot and a change-table with jars of lotion and baby oil. A bright mobile dangling from the ceiling, a small bookshelf crowded with cuddly toys bought by adoring friends and family.

She looked up, and Mark's dark eyes were watching her with unnerving intensity.

'I thought it would make a great nursery, too,' he said.

'You did?'

He lifted his hand and touched the side of her face with his fingertips, sending a warm glow through her like a sunrise.

He dipped his head so that his mouth was close to her ear. 'I can see it all. This room with soft, filmy curtains and fresh paint. Lush carpet. You in bed beside me.'

His deep, low voice sent a fresh rash of thrills rippling under Sophie's skin.

'Our baby sound asleep close by,' he murmured.

She would have been happy in a swag with Mark, but she had to admit he painted a very tempting picture—this room transformed, and her curled close beside him with her head on his shoulder, her arm flung possessively across his broad, bare chest and their legs entwined.

And their sweet little baby, a plump cutie with pink cheeks and a soft cap of dark hair, asleep in this little room right next to them...

Mark's hands spanned her waist; his lips brushed her skin. He kissed her temple, kissed the crease at the corner of her eye, trailed warm, soft lips down her cheek. And her skin turned to fire wherever his mouth touched her.

His big, work-toughened hand covered her abdomen and he caressed it gently with slow, tantalising strokes. 'You're going to be a terrific mother.'

'And you'll be a wonderful dad.'

'Our baby's a lucky little guy or girl.'

He grinned at her from beneath lowered black lashes. 'How long will it be before we find out what sex it is?'

'I'm not sure. A few weeks yet.'

Wrapping his arms around her, he drew her hard against him, gently rubbing the side of her face with his chin. 'I'm starting to get quite excited about this parenthood caper.'

'Me, too.'

'I have a very good feeling that we're going to manage just fine, Sophie.'

Slipping an arm around her shoulders and another beneath her knees, he lifted her easily and carried her to his bed, and she wondered if it was possible to feel any happier than she did right at that moment.

CHAPTER TEN

As soon as Jill Jackson heard that Sophie was staying on, she began to make plans. 'Now listen,' she told Mark when he answered the phone a couple of days later. 'I know we're jumping the gun here, but you'd better warn Sophie to prepare for an invasion.'

'I hope that's a friendly invasion?'

'Of course.' Jill laughed. 'Sue Matthews and Carrie Roper and I want to come over for a girls-only lunch. We'll bring the food, so Sophie doesn't have to lift a finger. We think it's high time she got to know more of her neighbours.'

Mark relayed the message to Sophie.

'Oh, wow!' Her face was an instant snapshot of delight. 'How kind of them. That's fabulous.'

Covering the mouthpiece, he asked her quietly, 'Are you sure you're not too tired? I could put them off till another day.' He'd been worried when he'd woken this morning and seen how pale she looked. There were mauve shadows under her eyes.

'I'm fine, Mark.'

With some reluctance, he relayed this to Jill.

'Wonderful,' Jill said. 'Now, Mark, you'll oblige us

by making yourself scarce, won't you? You can find a bore to mend, or something else useful. We girls are going to need plenty of time for a good old gossip.'

'What's this, secret women's business?'

'Exactly.'

'I can't believe they're going to so much trouble,' Sophie said after Mark hung up. 'They've got to travel so far!'

'Friendship's important out here.' He cupped her chin and looked into her face and felt a beat of fear, a dip in his pulse, like the shadow of a black crow's wing. 'I hope this lunch won't be too much for you.'

Sophie shook her head. 'If the women are bringing the food, I won't have to do much besides set the table.' She went to the stove, put the kettle on, then smiled back at him. 'Now this is why we need to do something about your dining room.'

'Point taken. Are you going to tell Jill and the girls about the baby?'

'I'd like to,' she said. 'Is it OK with you?'

'Sure. Women love to talk about babies, and if they know you're pregnant they'll understand that you should take things easy.'

'More importantly, they can tell me exactly what I need to know about the doctors and the hospital here.'

Whether it was presentiment, intuition, whatever... Mark felt a vague sense of unease as he kissed Sophie goodbye. He wished she didn't look quite so tired, but he wasn't planning on going too far today and he had no plausible excuse for hanging around. So he left her, taking a packed lunch and giving her his assurance that he would stay away until mid-afternoon so the women had plenty of time to chat.

It was about two o'clock, when he was in the middle of mending a leaky bore, that he heard the drone of an approaching plane. Looking up, he saw it dipping low as it came towards him. And then it waggled its wings, first port and then starboard.

He felt a shock of fright. It was the flying doctor's plane and it was never normally this low. It was a message. *Something was wrong!*

Instantly, he knew.

Sophie. Oh, God, Sophie.

His stomach turned to concrete.

Abandoning his task, he left his tools scattered as he ran two hundred metres to the truck. Why the hell had he left the phone in the truck? He should have had it with him.

As he ran, his mind threw up crazy possibilities. Sophie had sliced her hand with a kitchen knife. She'd been bitten by a snake. A red-back spider. Or maybe it was the food those women had brought. Food poisoning?

It couldn't be something to do with the baby. Fear clutched at his throat, strangled him.

Don't let anything happen to the baby. Please, no.

His hands shook as he reached for the phone. He didn't bother to listen to messages, but dialled straight to Coolabah Waters.

Jill Jackson answered.

'What's happened?' Mark yelled. 'Is Sophie all right?'

'Mark, the flying doctors have taken her to Mount Isa hospital. She started having cramps. I knew you were out at the bore, but we couldn't get you on the phone so I asked the pilot to buzz you.'

She spoke quietly and calmly, but Mark wasn't deceived. Jill was a trained nurse and her calm manner was bluff.

'Cramps!' he cried. 'What's that mean? A miscarriage?'

'Not necessarily, but Sophie also started to bleed,' Jill said.

A cry of horror broke from Mark. 'I'm on my way.'

He careered across the plains at break-neck speed and he cursed at every gate. Cursed himself for leaving the sat phone in the truck and for leaving Sophie at home. He'd known this morning that something was wrong.

He even snapped at Monty, on the seat beside him. The cattle dog hunkered low and let out a whine.

It seemed to take for ever to reach the home paddock. Scorching across the final hundred metres, he pulled up in a cloud of red dust at the bottom of the back steps.

Jill Jackson was waiting for him, and the grim set of her face confirmed his worst fears. She hurried down the stairs as he leapt out of the truck.

'Don't panic, Mark,' she said, laying a cool hand on his arm.

Don't panic? How the hell could he *not* panic? Mark's head swam and his stomach pitched.

'Mark, sit down,' Jill said. 'You look like you're going to faint.'

Before he could deny this, he was dragged to the steps. Two hands on his shoulders pushed him down until his butt came into contact with a timber slab.

'I'm OK,' he protested. 'I've never fainted in my life.'

Ignoring him, Jill set her hand on the back of his

neck and gently but firmly held his head down between his knees.

'I know what you men are like. Andrew's just as bad. When you're dealing with men and cattle, you're the toughest guys in the west. But you should have seen Andrew trying to keep up a brave face when I was in labour.'

'I've got to go to her.' Mark jerked his head up, saw the paddocks swim before him, and Jill pushed him down again.

'You can't drive anywhere just yet, but you'll be all right in a minute. You just need to get over the shock and have a cup of tea.'

'For crying out loud!' This time Mark jumped to his feet. Dizziness threatened, but he ignored it. 'I don't need a tea party.'

If Sophie was in trouble, there was no way he would waste time sipping tea.

Looking up, he saw Sophie's other guests, Sue Matthews and Carrie Roper, peering anxiously from the back doorway.

'It's such a shame,' called Carrie. 'Such a shock for poor Sophie the way it happened. There we were, chatting away about hospitals and labour, when Sophie laughed and said she was having sympathy pains. No one dreamed…'

A warning glance from Jill stopped Carrie in mid-track.

'Thanks to all of you for looking after Sophie,' Mark said bleakly. 'I'll be off now.'

'What about taking a shower?' suggested Sue.

'And you might need some clean clothes,' said Carrie.

He brusquely waved these suggestions aside and ran

to the shed where the Range Rover was parked. It would be quicker on the highway than the truck, and more comfortable for bringing Sophie home again.

'Take care, Mark,' Jill called after him. 'Don't be an idiot on the road. Sophie needs you in one piece.'

It was more than two hundred kilometres to Mount Isa, and Mark tore over the distance at a punishing pace. He was *burning* to get to Sophie.

He tried not to think about what might be happening to her, couldn't bear to think she might be losing the baby—or worse, that her own life was in danger.

Surely not? Sophie was young and strong, healthy and vibrant.

His mind was a turmoil of recriminations.

Hell. I shouldn't have let her take on so much.

But she'd seemed so well.

I shouldn't have made love to her. How could I have forgotten her delicate condition?

But she'd been so eager.

What could he do? He felt so useless, trapped in this vehicle, tormented by his imagination, angered beyond reason by the miles of bitumen that separated them.

He blinked as the road in front of him blurred. Damn. No sense in falling apart. He had to keep his head. But how was a guy supposed to stay calm in a situation like this? He'd rather face a stampede single-handed than see Sophie in a hospital bed.

At last, at the hospital, they directed Mark to Sophie's ward.

Uneasily aware of waxed linoleum and the smell of

antiseptic, he stepped out of the lift onto her floor and made his way down a long hallway.

He caught a glimpse of his reflection in a glass door. Damn it, Sue and Carrie had been right. He should have showered and changed before dashing here straight from the dirty work of fixing a bore. Normally, he'd never think of coming to town in this condition.

When he stopped at a nurses' station and asked again for directions to Sophie Felsham, the nurse studied him over half-moon glasses. For the first time in his life, he felt his confidence draining. He was so out of place here, so not in control.

'Sophie Felsham,' the nurse repeated, and she studied her clipboard, looked up again and narrowed her pale eyes at him. 'Are you her next of kin?'

'I—I'm her baby's father.'

Her lips pursed as she considered this and she looked again at the clipboard.

'Her family are all in England,' he said, raising his voice as his patience frayed.

Why can't they just tell me where Sophie is?

Mark had always been slow to anger, but the longer the nurse took to tell him what he needed to know, the more impatient he grew.

'You've got to tell me where I can find her!' he commanded, bringing a clenched fist down on the counter and sending a pen flying. The pen was chained to the counter top, but Mark wouldn't have cared if it had flown out of the window.

From her seat behind the counter, the nurse glared up at him.

Mark scowled down at her.

She said finally in a tone of faint dismissal, 'Room twenty-two.'

'Thank you,' Mark replied, resuming his usual polite and gentlemanly charm. About to leave, he paused. 'How—how is she?'

Perhaps the nurse saw his fear. Her face softened and she said more gently, 'I'm afraid you'll have to ask Sister Hart.'

'OK. Where is she?'

'Busy with another patient at the moment.'

He spun away, cursed under his breath, went in search of room twenty-two.

From the doorway he saw her.

Sophie was the only patient in the room, and she lay perfectly still with her eyes shut. There was a white square of sticking plaster on the back of her hand, as if a drip had been inserted at some stage.

Mark's heart juddered.

He sucked in a deep breath. *Pull yourself together, man.*

She didn't stir when he tiptoed carefully into the room and pulled out a chair. He sat beside her bed and waited, unnerved to find her asleep. Somehow he hadn't expected that. What did it mean? Was she terribly ill?

His throat ached, and he couldn't swallow. He watched the gentle rise and fall of her chest beneath the crisp white sheet, admired the sheen on her shiny dark hair as it caught the bright overhead lights, loved the way her eyelashes lay against her pale cheeks. He saw the delicate tracery of blue veins on her eyelids and the soft, pink lushness of her lips. He thought she'd never looked more beautiful.

But so alone.

Removed from him.

His gaze dropped to his dusty jeans and boots. There was a black grease-mark on his wrist and he rubbed it against his denim thigh, trying to clean it.

Perhaps the movement disturbed Sophie. She opened her eyes. 'Mark!'

He tried for a smile and missed. 'Hey there, beautiful girl.'

'How long have you been here?'

'Five minutes.' He leaned closer. 'How are you?'

Her face crumpled and she shook her head. She squashed three fingers against her quivering mouth, as if to stop herself from crying, but her lovely eyes glittered and tears spilled.

'Sweetheart.'

She gave a helpless shake of her head.

Mark didn't know what to say, what to ask, how to touch her. He patted her hand, fingered a strand of her hair. 'You sure know how to frighten a guy.'

This time he managed a weak smile.

But it didn't help Sophie. She began to sob and, no matter how hard she pressed her hand over her mouth, the sobs broke through.

Terrified and uncertain, conscious of his dusty clothes, Mark leaned close and tried to kiss her cheek.

Her arms encircled his neck. She clung to him, and her body shook violently with the force of her sobbing.

'You poor girl.' What could he say? What *should* he say? 'Don't worry.'

'I l-lost the b-baby!'

Mark's stomach dropped...and it kept falling and falling...

No baby.

He choked back an exclamation, a groan of despair. His job was to reassure Sophie, not to add to her anguish.

But the baby? Their little bean— Gone?

Another shock jolted through him and then an awful sense of loss pressed down, suffocating him, and he had to take huge gulps of air. *Hell.* If he felt this bad, how much worse must it be for poor Sophie?

She was weeping uncontrollably. He kissed her damp cheek and wished he could find the right words to comfort her. He held her, tried to soothe her, rocked her gently as he would a small child.

At last her storm of crying began to ease.

She sniffed noisily. 'I'm so sorry, Mark.'

'Shh.' It killed him that she felt a need to apologise. He lifted a box of tissues from the stand beside her bed. 'Here.'

Her eyes and nose were pink from crying. She took a handful of tissues, mopped at her face and blew her nose. 'Have they told you what happened?'

'Not a word. All I know is what Jill could tell me.'

Sophie gave a shaky sigh and sank back onto her pillow. 'As soon as I got here they did a scan,' she said. 'And they discovered that the baby—the—the foetus— had stopped developing.'

Her mouth pulled out of shape as she struggled to hold back another burst of tears. 'All this time I— I've been thinking about my little bean…our little baby growing into…' She stopped, closed her eyes and drew a deep, shuddering breath.

When she opened her eyes again, she said in a flat, exhausted voice, 'It was never going to happen. I've had what they call an inevitable miscarriage.'

Inevitable.

All this time, there'd been no chance of a baby.

'The doctor said it was just one of those things,' Sophie added. 'He said there's usually no explanation, but it's very common.'

Mark swallowed. 'Right.'

'And so that's that.' She sank miserably back onto her pillow and closed her eyes, and Mark saw again the blue-veined lids, the curling lashes. 'It's all over, Mark.'

It was like being cast adrift without a mooring rope.

Mark groped for words of reassurance, but could only find trite platitudes.

Grimly quiet, with her eyes still closed, Sophie said, 'It's "as you were" now. Everything's back to normal.'

Suddenly he sensed the direction of her thoughts. 'No!'

Sophie's eyes flashed open and she looked directly at him. 'I've been such a bother to you. I should never have rushed down here and thrown your life into chaos.'

'Have—have I ever complained?'

'No.' She laid her hand very lightly on his arm. 'You're a good man, Mark.'

'A good man'? Had any words been more dismissive? That was what people said at funerals—when they were saying goodbye. For ever.

Sophie's eyes were bright with a tough battle-light Mark had never seen before.

'You can go home to Coolabah Waters and get on with your life,' she said.

CHAPTER ELEVEN

THERE. She'd done it. The dreadful words that set Mark free had flowed from her in a painful rush, the way the baby had.

And she was left with the same desolate emptiness.

It was like ripping her heart out, but now, at the lowest point in her life, Sophie knew she had no choice. She had to face up to her most difficult challenge yet.

From the moment the mean, cramping pain had begun low in her abdomen, she'd known that she was losing the baby. And she'd known that meant losing Mark. She'd had plenty of time to think about it—in the plane on the way to the hospital, and later with tears rolling down her cheeks as the hospital staff had examined her and dealt with the miscarriage.

Afterwards, she'd wanted nothing more than to curl in a ball, to give in to her grief and the tumult of her hormones, to feel desperately sorry for herself. Yet again. But the funny thing about love was that it wouldn't let you be selfish. And, in the depths of her misery, she'd realised it was time to think about Mark for a change.

Poor Mark. She'd rushed down here and made a mess

of his life. She'd distracted him from important work by insisting that he show her his lifestyle.

She'd been so thoughtless. Even their love-making— Oh, *help,* how could she ever forget Mark's love-making? But even then, she'd been selfish. One minute she'd been holding him at bay, telling him that sex would complicate everything, next she was leaping into his swag.

She'd been too focused on her own problems for too long, too scared of failing yet again. But now it was time to grow up.

If she was brutally honest, she'd known from the start that Mark was a gentleman, too well-mannered to simply send her packing even though he'd probably wanted to. And Tim, Emma and her mum had all made their expectations clear to him. Everyone back in England was hoping Mark would 'do the right thing' and somehow save Sophie from yet another failure.

She'd failed anyhow. Life had taught her a huge and terrible lesson. She'd failed spectacularly. She'd lost the baby, the one thing that she and Mark had in common. The *only* thing tying him to her. And, after all the burdens she'd piled on the poor man, it was up to her to make things easier for him now.

It had to be done. Sophie knew she had no choice but to release Mark from any sense of obligation, had to be convincing for his sake.

If only he didn't look so ill. Beneath his tan, his skin had taken on a sickly pallor. His dark-brown eyes were glazed with shock.

And, although the muscles in his throat worked overtime, he didn't speak. He wouldn't look at her, and simply stared at the foot of her bed.

Don't do this to me, Mark. Don't make it too hard.

Eventually, he said, 'Are you saying goodbye? You want to split?'

'Yes.' She was proud of how definite that one awful word sounded.

'But you'll come home with me first?'

Sophie, be brave.

'No, Mark. There's no need.'

'So—so after they let you out of here you plan to head straight back to England?'

'Of course.' She knew this sounded too harsh, so she added more gently, 'As soon as I can organise a flight.'

Mark's jaw clenched, and he shifted his point of focus to another part of her bed, but still he didn't look at her.

'It's a bit of a nuisance that I've left so much stuff at your place,' she said. 'Would it be too much to ask you to box it up and send it over?'

'I'll go home and get it tonight,' he said dully.

'But it's such a long way.'

His jaw clenched harder, and he spoke through gritted teeth. 'I'm used to long distances.'

Sophie felt sick at the thought of Mark driving back through the dark, over those long, lonely miles. Her throat burned with welling tears, but she didn't want to cry again. If she burst into tears, he'd never believe that she wanted to go. Besides, she'd cried too much already.

Mark said, 'Do you really think we can do this—just part as easily as we did in London, after the wedding?' His voice was hard and cold, as if he'd chipped each word from a block of ice

She couldn't trust herself to speak, so she nodded,

and she felt as if she might fall apart completely at any moment.

Mark leaned closer, his voice bitter-quiet. 'I can't believe you think we can say goodbye, as if nothing important has happened between us.'

Important?

Was that what he thought? What did he mean by that, was he just talking about sex?

Mark's hand gripped her shoulder. 'Tell me you don't mean it, Sophie.' His voice was too loud, almost angry.

'Is everything all right, Sophie?'

A woman's stern voice startled her. Through her tears, Sophie saw the nursing sister standing behind Mark.

Sophie nodded. 'Yes, I'm fine, thanks.' But her voice was squeaky and trembling. She groped for the ball of tissues under her pillow and dabbed at her face.

The nurse gave Mark a baleful look. 'She's obviously upset. I'll have to ask you to leave.'

'He's not upsetting me,' Sophie insisted.

'Just the same, I'll ask you step outside, sir. I need to check Sophie's progress. This will only take a moment.'

Outside, in the corridor, Mark wondered if he was losing his mind. He was free to go, but nothing about that felt right. What was wrong with him? Why did he feel so bad? Most bachelors in his position would have been relieved, wouldn't they?

He'd been let off the hook, and he was free to pick up his life where he'd left off when the young jackaroo had announced a long-distance phone call from a woman with an English accent.

Sophie Felsham was not going to make her home at Coolabah Waters after all. And he wasn't going to be a father. The burden of responsibility had rolled from his shoulders, and he was free to marry any girl he chose.

He should be pleased, shouldn't he? Wasn't this their lucky break—*his* lucky break?

There were unlimited Australian women who would slip into his lifestyle much more easily than Sophie could. Surely providence had intervened and had delivered them both from a life sentence?

But if that was the case why in blue blazes didn't he feel relieved?

The raw ache in the pit of his stomach, the numbness in his heart, didn't make sense. Shouldn't he feel the tiniest glimmer of hope about his future?

Hands plunged in pockets, he strode to the far end of the corridor, and glared out at the car park where windscreens flashed gold in the harsh blaze of the setting sun.

He didn't want an Australian girl. He didn't want anyone else.

That was the crazy truth of it. He wanted Sophie— bright, lovely, gutsy Sophie.

But fate had intervened and turned the clock back. They were just a man and woman again. There was no pregnancy. No possible son and heir. No cute baby girl. No chance that his bedroom would be decorated with rosy accents, whatever they were. No nursery…

Their lives had been stripped back to the basics. All that was left was how he and Sophie felt about each other.

And Sophie had already made her feelings crystal clear.

Turning from the window, he stared back down the long white corridor.

He couldn't believe how much it hurt that she wanted to rush back to England. It wasn't as if she had hated it at Coolabah. Already she'd made a terrific fist of settling into the Outback. She'd thrown everything she had into learning how to adapt, had shown the courageous spirit of the Englishwomen who'd pioneered this hard land.

And there'd been many times when he'd caught her looking at him, had seen in her eyes that she cared for him. *Really* cared. And she'd made love with heart-wrenching eagerness, with a depth of passion that couldn't be faked.

Damn it, there'd been every indication that they could have been happy together here.

You're fooling yourself, mate. If Sophie wanted to stay, she wouldn't hesitate to say so.

She's desperate to get back to England.

His hand balled into a fist. He wanted to smash something. But, damn it, if England was where Sophie truly wanted to be, he had no right to keep her here. He'd told her she was free to go if things didn't work out.

And, well…things hadn't worked out.

End of story.

She was the daughter of Sir Kenneth and Lady Eliza. She belonged in London with them, with Emma and Tim.

But how the hell could he let her go?

He couldn't.

It was as simple as that. Yes!

He couldn't let her go. He wasn't convinced that Sophie really wanted to walk away from him. After everything they'd shared, it didn't make sense. He had questions to ask. He had to know for sure.

He set off down the corridor with a quickened step and a fiercely brave heart.

The nurse was just leaving the room.

'I've given Sophie a sedative to help her calm down,' she said, casting a dubious eye over Mark. 'I think it would be best if we leave her now. She mustn't be upset. She needs plenty of rest.'

'I'll just say goodbye,' he insisted.

But when he stepped through the doorway Sophie was lying curled on her side, with her back to him, and when he leaned over the bed she didn't move. Her eyes were shut, her eyelids red and swollen, and her hands were folded, clutching a bunch of damp tissues beneath her chin. She looked as if she might be praying.

She looked pale and exhausted, but the message was clear: she wasn't expecting or seeking any comfort from him.

In the car park he rang Jill.

'What a dreadful shame, Mark. Poor Sophie. Poor you.'

'I guess it's just one of those things that happen,' he said.

'Yes, of course. It happens a lot, actually. And I'm sure Sophie will have more babies.'

Mark cleared his throat. 'I—I guess so.'

'Just the same, it's a terrible disappointment for you both,' she said. 'And such a frightening experience for the poor girl.'

'I'm grateful you were there to help her.'

'Yes, so am I. Does she have enough things? I packed a small overnight bag for her.'

'I'm coming back to collect what she needs. I don't want to hang around in Mount Isa tonight, so I'll grab a hamburger and coffee at a service station and I can be home by ten.'

'You're coming back out here tonight?'

Jill was clearly puzzled by this, but Mark finished the conversation quickly and disconnected. He couldn't bring himself to tell her about Sophie's plans to return to London. He still couldn't believe them himself.

He tackled the task of gathering up Sophie's things as soon as he got back. 'Stressful' didn't go halfway to describing the ordeal. He was dog-tired, but too tense to sleep, so he went to the back bedroom, dragged out her suitcase from beneath the bed and began to pack.

He went about the task with grim thoroughness, taking care to put shoes and heavy things like jeans towards the bottom. He opened the drawer where Sophie kept her underwear. A hint of her scent still lingered, and his hands shook as he packed silken panties, lacy bras and her soft cotton nightdress. Every garment, each item, conjured memories that tore his heart to shreds.

On the little table in the corner of the room, he discovered pages torn from a notebook—a pen-and-ink sketch of his bedroom with notes about furniture and suggestions for colours, fabric and carpets. On the page beneath it, a sketch of the little nursery.

Sophie had drawn in details here: an old-fashioned timber cot, a patchwork quilt, a rug for the floor, a rocking chair and cupboard, shelves for stuffed toys, the small round window.

Mark stared at the simple drawings and wanted to hurl himself down on the floor and howl like a child.

He was losing her. Losing Sophie and her baby. Losing everything.

With an anguished groan, he tossed the pages of sketches on top of her folded clothes and fled her room.

But he knew that his bedroom couldn't offer him any peace either, not with memories of Sophie sharing it with him.

Tense as fencing wire, he flung open the door of the linen press, dragged out a blanket and pillow. He would make do with the sofa tonight.

He was hauling off his boots when the phone rang. Leaping up, he stumbled over them in his hurry to answer it.

Please, let it be Sophie!

'Hello. Is that Mark?'

He suppressed a groan. An English accent, but not Sophie's. Her mother's.

Hell! He was going to have to tell her the news.

'Hello, Lady Eliza.'

'I'm sorry to be ringing so late, Mark. I tried earlier, but you weren't home.'

'No worries. I wasn't asleep.' He dragged in a ragged breath. 'But I'm afraid Sophie's not here. She's—'

Damn. He was in danger of breaking down. He pinched the bridge of his nose as he struggled for control.

'Sophie's in hospital. I'm afraid she's had a miscarriage.'

'Oh, Mark.' Lady Eliza's voice trembled.

'She—she's OK. Just resting overnight.'

'My poor baby. I've had this dreadful feeling all day that something was wrong with her. That's why I've been trying to call.'

There was a tiny silence.

'I'm so sorry, Mark. When Sophie told me about the

pregnancy, she sounded so happy. Confident and self-assured. I thought it was wonderful news. She said you were really happy about the baby, too.'

'Yeah.' Mark couldn't hold back a heavy sigh. He leaned a shoulder against the kitchen wall. 'But the doctors said it was inevitable. The foetus had stopped developing.'

'I see. Well, these things happen, of course. But it's very disappointing. Poor Sophie. She'll need some tender loving care when she gets back home with you.'

Mark swallowed. 'She's not coming back here.'

'I beg your pardon?'

'She's heading back to London.'

In the stunned silence that followed, Mark gritted his teeth, and squeezed his eyes tightly shut.

'Mark,' Lady Eliza said at last. 'I know it's none of my business, but are you happy with Sophie's decision?'

Oh God. His throat was so tight he didn't think he could speak.

'I know my daughter, Mark. She's very impulsive and inclined to overreact, and I don't suppose she's had much time to think this through.'

'Not really.'

'You're upset, aren't you?'

'This has been the worst day of my life.'

'Would it would help to talk?'

'I doubt it.'

But he knew it would happen anyway. There was something very kind and compelling about Sophie's mother. With another deep sigh, Mark lowered himself to the floor, sat with his back against the wall.

'OK,' he said, closing his eyes again as tears stung. 'What do you think we should do?'

* * *

The doctor was quite jovial when he saw Sophie on his rounds the next morning. 'Now, just remember, there is nothing wrong with your reproductive system,' he told her. 'You should put this behind you. I'm sure you'll be able to go full-term with your next pregnancy. And the other good news is you're fine to go home.'

Home. Her mind flashed to Coolabah Waters. But she had to scratch that thought. Home, of course, was her London flat. Sophie pictured it and waited for the appropriate rush of nostalgia.

Nothing happened.

Maybe she would feel more excited when she got back to England, when she saw her mother and Emma, when she was among her own things.

Maybe then she would be able to delete pictures of a tall, dark and handsome cattleman, and of wide, brown plains and a low house with an iron roof.

Once she was safely home she could put this episode behind her. In time, her memories of Mark Winchester and Coolabah Waters would fade like a bad dream.

Bad dream?

Who was she trying to kid?

Everything about Mark was perfect. She'd never forget him, never stop missing him. She'd fallen completely and totally in love with the man. In spite of his mysterious Outback.

Actually, there was every chance she was halfway in love with the Outback, too. After all, it was a part of Mark. And she'd known all along that Mark and his lifestyle were a package deal. Regrettably, now, it seemed that she loved them both.

As she threw her things into the overnight bag that

Jill had packed for her, she wondered if there were enough words in the dictionary to describe how wretched she felt. She placed her hand over her stomach, over her *flat*, empty womb that had been denied the chance to finish its task.

She wanted it full to bursting, longed for her little bean, fat and healthy, growing into a naughty, lively, little boy or girl.

Her knees buckled and she sank to the edge of the bed. It was so hard to accept there was nothing now. There never had been a chance of a baby being born.

It was even harder to accept that the end of her pregnancy meant losing Mark. But she could hardly pretend that he would have considered a long-term relationship with her if it hadn't been for the baby.

When he'd made love to her, he'd whispered endearments so sweet they'd thrilled her to the bone, and had encouraged her to hope that he loved her. But he'd never repeated them in the cold light of day.

There was no avoiding the truth. Mark wouldn't expect or want her to stay on without the baby. Yesterday's decision to leave had nearly killed her, but deep down she knew it was the right, the only thing to do. This morning, she had to find the quickest way to get back to England.

Mark was halfway down the highway when his phone rang.

'Mark, it's Sophie. I'm so glad I got through to you.'

Goosebumps broke out on his arms and back. 'Where are you? I tried to ring you at the hospital, but they said you'd checked out.'

'Yes. I'm fighting fit, apparently. I'm in a coffee shop in the main part of town. Where are you?'

'About an hour away. I've packed the rest of your things and I have them with me.'

'That's so kind of you.'

Kind? No, not kind—crazy!

'I've rung the airlines and booked my flights,' she said.

Mark swore. Hoped Sophie didn't hear it. The goose-bumps morphed into a cold sweat. 'When—uh—when are you planning to leave?'

'I've a flight to the coast that leaves around twelve.'

Twelve? He gripped the steering wheel so tightly, his knuckles almost snapped. 'Why? Why the rush?'

'I'll spend a couple of nights in Sydney,' she said, neatly avoiding his question. 'I can fly home on Friday.'

'But isn't that too soon? Don't you need a little more time to—to get over everything?'

'I'll be OK. It's best this way.'

Best? Sophie had to be joking. It was the worst news possible. But there was no sense in having an argument with her when he was in the middle of the highway.

'I'll be cutting it a bit fine, but I'll make it,' he told her.

'I shouldn't keep you on the phone if you're driving, Mark. I'll head over to the airport and meet you there. See you in about an hour.'

'Wait!' he shouted. 'We need to talk, Sophie. It's important…'

But she'd already disconnected.

In the ladies' room in the airport, Sophie stood in front of the mirror. She was wearing the clothes Jill had packed for her, a purple T-shirt with a scooped neck and a short

denim skirt. But in the harsh light of the overhead fluo-
rescent tube she looked like a dying heroine in the final
act of one of her mother's tragic operas.

Just thinking about her mother brought tears to her
eyes. Last night she'd wanted to phone her, but she
hadn't felt brave enough to tell her that everything had
gone wrong, that she'd failed again.

She rubbed concealer into the shadows under her
eyes, used a tinted moisturiser to blend everything
together, added a little blush and some lip gloss, and
then sifted her fingers through her hair in an attempt to
plump up her curls.

She tried to smile at her reflection.

Come on, Sophie, you can do better than that.

Taking several deep breaths, she tried again. *Cringe!*
She looked like a clown, with an artificially smiling
mouth and tragic eyes.

She tried to picture Mark striding into the terminal—
her tall, strapping heartthrob in blue jeans. Her smile
held until she got to the part where they began to say
goodbye, and the reflection in the mirror cracked and
crumpled. A glint of silver sparkled in her eyes.

No, no! She was not going to cry today. She had to
steel herself. She was going to get through this. She
would say farewell to Mark with a brave smile and
without shedding a single tear.

She went to the airport kiosk. Her nerves were too
on edge for more coffee, so she bought a magazine and
a bottle of water, found a comfortable chair and sat
down and pretended to read.

It didn't work, of course. The magazine was full of
stories about celebrities with relationship problems. What

did she care about their heartache when her own was off the scale? She turned to the crossword. The answers to the first few clues were easy, so she scribbled them in.

This was better; if she concentrated on the crossword, she might be able to forget about…

Zap!

Sophie dropped her pen as long jeans-clad legs and brown elastic-sided boots entered her line of sight.

Her head jerked up and there was Mark, wearing a white long-sleeved shirt that showed off his tan, and looking a million times more gorgeous than any film star. Her heart began to race.

But then she saw his eyes, and the dark pain there made her so suddenly weak she was sure she would never get out of her chair.

'You made good time,' she said, trying to smile at him and failing miserably.

She couldn't think what to say next, knew that neither of them was in the mood for small talk.

Mark set her suitcase down, and she groped for her handbag on the seat beside her.

'I just need my passport,' she said, fishing in an inside pocket. 'And then I can check in.'

As she feared, her legs were wobbly when she tried to stand. Mark was beside her in an instant, his hand at her elbow, supporting her.

'Sophie, this is crazy. You're in no condition to be setting out on a long journey.'

She threw back her shoulders, pinned on a smile and tried hard to ignore the electrifying thrill of his hand on her arm. 'I'm fine, Mark. And I have two nights in Sydney before the long haul home.'

Gripping her other arm, he pulled her around so that she faced him, and his eyes blazed with an intensity that frightened her.

He spoke through tight lips. 'Tell me honestly that this is what you want.'

Startled, she cried, 'Of course it's what I want!' She willed herself to mean it, and couldn't let herself think otherwise, not for a fraction of a second.

'Honestly!' Mark hissed, gripping her harder. 'If you have even a shadow of a doubt about going home, say so now, Sophie.'

This was so unlike Mark. She waggled her passport in his face. 'There's no reason for me to stay now. You know that. You can get on with your life.'

'That's rubbish.' Still he gripped her. 'You haven't said it.'

Her throat was so full she couldn't breathe. Her vision blurred.

'Sophie.' Mark held her arms more tightly than ever. 'Can you really tell me that you can walk away with no regrets at all?'

She blinked to stop herself from weeping.

Mark stood very still, looking down at her with a face that seemed to be carved from stone. Except for his eyes. His eyes burned her.

'Don't for one moment imagine that I am free to get on with my life,' he said quietly. 'Not without you.'

'B-but there's no baby.'

'I know, and I'm really sorry about that, sweetheart.' Without warning, Mark loosened his grip, let his hands slide down her arms until he held her loosely at the wrists. 'Sophie, I'm very sorry there's just the two of us now. I mourn the loss of our baby more than you can possibly guess.'

The tears she'd been battling sprang into her eyes and trembled on the ends of her lashes.

'But don't you see what losing the baby means?' Mark gave her hands a gentle shake. 'This is only about *us* now. It's about how I feel about you, Sophie Felsham. You alone. And I'm telling you I can't let you get on that plane. I know I'll never see you again. And I—I can't bear to lose you.'

She stood very still, saw how very nervous Mark was, saw the unguarded truth in his eyes.

'Tell me, Sophie, short of throwing myself on the tarmac in front of the plane, what have I got to do?' He released her and held out his hands, offered her a disarming, trembling smile. 'There's nothing I won't do to keep you.'

She hardly dared to believe her ears. Each word Mark uttered was like a healing balm for her unravelled heart.

'I love you,' he said. 'What else can I say to persuade you to stay?'

'Oh Mark.' She gave him a weepy grin as she stumbled forward and reached for his hands. 'I think you've already said it.'

'I mean it, Sophie. I love you. I know you've had a man tell you this before, then turn around and hurt you. But I swear I mean it, darling. I'm not going to change my mind about loving you. You do understand that, don't you?

'Yes,' she said softly. 'I understand, Mark. It's almost too good to be true, but I do understand.'

'I love you so much, Sophie. I can't let you go. I don't believe I can live without you.'

Sophie lifted Mark's hand to her cheek, and it felt strong and good and wonderful. Steadfast.

'I know I'm asking a lot to expect you to live with me at Coolabah Waters,' he said. 'It's hardly the Ritz.'

'I don't want the Ritz, Mark. The Outback is an acquired taste, but it's growing on me fast. I'm not so sure that I belong in London any more. I was actually feeling very miserable at the thought of going back there.'

Heedless of the travellers milling about them, Mark gathered her in and kissed her with infinite tenderness.

Speaking softly so that only she could hear, he said, 'Ever since you arrived here, I've been falling more deeply in love with you. Every morning, every night, all day long. I would never have believed it's quite, quite possible to fall hopelessly, painfully in love in less than fortnight.'

'I believe.' Deeply moved, she touched her fingers to his lips. 'The same thing has happened to me.'

His face flooded with a smile as bright as the Australian sun.

'I promise I'll make you happy if you stay, Sophie.'

He cupped her face and they kissed, slowly, deeply.

Against his lips, Sophie whispered, 'I love you, too.' And then, 'Let's go home,' she said, eagerly linking her arm through Mark's.

'Best idea yet.'

They were halfway to the car when they remembered her suitcase, still sitting where Mark had left it in the middle of the terminal building.

Laughing, they hurried back to collect it. 'I almost forgot something else,' Mark said as he put the case in the back of the Range Rover. 'Your mother rang last night.'

'Really? What did she want?'

'She was worried about her baby daughter. Had a gut feeling that something was wrong.'

'Goodness.' Sophie marvelled at how warmed she was by her mum's unexpected concern. 'That's nice to know.'

'I told her what had happened, and she was terribly sorry and we had rather a long chat. I ended up inviting her out here for a visit.'

Sophie's jaw dropped. 'My mum wouldn't be able to come. She's always far too busy.'

Mark shook his head. 'She's coming all right. It's mid-season for the opera company, but she said her understudy will be delighted at the chance to sing this role.'

'Wow!' Sophie felt unbelievably chuffed to think her mother wanted to come all this way just to see her. But as she took this in a more puzzling thought struck. 'But—but how could you have invited her, when you didn't even know I was going to stay?'

'I guess...' Mark shrugged and smiled shyly. 'I wouldn't allow myself to consider the alternative.'

'Oh, Mark!'

'She'll be here in two days' time, and I thought it would be really nice if she could help co-ordinate our wedding.'

Sophie couldn't hold back a shriek of excitement. Tears flowed down her cheeks as she threw her arms about Mark and gave him an ecstatic hug. 'That is the most beautiful, beautiful suggestion I've ever heard.'

He rewarded her with a long, hard kiss.

Eventually, when they got into the vehicle and Sophie secured her seatbelt, she remembered another important piece of news. 'The doctor said we can try again for a baby in a month or two.'

Mark smiled. 'Of course we can. We can have a whole tribe of them.'

'I think I'd like to call our first baby Jack.'

'Jack Winchester?' He grinned as he fitted the key into the ignition. 'Sounds good, but what's wrong with Jane?'

'Nothing,' smiled Sophie. 'I'll settle for either.'

'We'll have both,' he said as he accelerated out of the car park.

And, as they turned and headed for home, Sophie saw no reason to doubt him.

* * * * *

"Welcome to the family, Briton," said one of Olaf's men in a mocking voice. "We look forward to the presence of a woman at our hall."

Bronwen grasped her tunic and yanked it from the Viking's thick fingers. As she stepped away from the table, she heard the drunken laughter of the barbarians behind her. How could her father have betrothed her to the old Viking?

Running down the stone steps toward the heavy oak door that led outside from the keep, Bronwen gathered her mantle about her. She ordered the doorman to open the door, and he did so reluctantly, pressing her to carry a torch. But Bronwen pushed past him and fled into the darkness.

Dashing down the steep, pebbled hill toward the beach, she felt the frozen ground give way to sand. She threw off her veil and circlet and kicked away her shoes.

Racing alongside the pounding surf, she felt hot tears of anger and shame well up and stream down her cheeks. With no concern for her safety, Bronwen ran and ran—her long braids streaming behind her, falling loose, drifting like a tattered black flag.

Blinded with weeping, she did not see the dark form

that sprang up in her path and stopped dead her headlong sprint. Bronwen shrieked in surprise and fear as iron arms pinned her, and a heavy cloak threatened to suffocate her.

"Release me!" she cried. "Guard! Guard, help me."

"Hush, my lady." A deep voice emanated from the darkness. "I mean you no harm. What demon drives you to run through the night without fear for your safety?"

"Release me, villain! I am the daughter—"

"I shall hold you until you calm yourself. We had heard there were witches in Amounderness, but I had not thought to meet one so openly."

Still held tight in the man's arms, Bronwen drew back and peered up at the hooded figure. "You! You are the man who spied on our feast. Release me at once, or I shall call the guard upon you."

The man chuckled at this and turned toward his companions, who stood in a group nearby. Bronwen caught hold of the back of his hood and jerked it down to reveal a head of glossy raven curls. But the man's face was shrouded in darkness yet, and as he looked at her, she could not read his expression.

"So you are the blessed bride-to-be." He returned the hood to his head. "Your father has paired you with an interesting choice."

Relieved that her captor did not appear to be a highwayman, she pushed away from him and sagged onto the wet sand. "Please leave me here alone. I need peace to think. Go on your way."

The tall stranger shrugged off his outer mantle and wrapped it around her shoulders. "Why did your father betroth you thus to the aged Viking?" he asked.

"For one purported to be a spy, you know precious little about Amounderness. But I shall tell you, as it is all common knowledge."

She pulled the cloak tightly about her, reveling in its warmth. "This land, known as Amounderness, once was Briton territory. Olaf Lothbrok, my betrothed, came here as a youth when the Viking invasions had nearly subsided. He took the lands directly to the south of Rossall Hall from their Briton lord. Then, of course, the Normans came, and Amounderness was pillaged by William the Conqueror's army."

The man squatted on the sand beside Bronwen. He listened with obvious interest as she continued. "When William took an account of Amounderness in his Domesday Book, he recorded no remaining lords and few people at all. But he did not know the Britons. Slowly we crept out of hiding and returned to our halls. My father's family reoccupied Rossall Hall. And there we live, as we should, watching over our serfs as they fish and grow their meager crops. Indeed, there is not much here for the greedy Normans to want, if they are the ones for whom you spy."

Unwilling to continue speaking when her heart was so heavy, Bronwen stood and turned toward the sea. The traveler rose beside her and touched her arm. "Olaf Lothbrok's lands—together with your father's—will reunite most of Amounderness under the rule of the son you are beholden to bear. A clever plan. Your sister's future husband holds the rest of the adjoining lands, I understand."

"You've done your work, sir. Your lord will be pleased. Who is he—some land-hungry Scottish baron?

Or have you forgotten that King Stephen gave Amounderness to the Scots, as a trade for their support in his war with Matilda? I certainly hope your lord is not a Norman. He would be so disappointed to learn he has no legal rights here. Now, if you will excuse me?"

Bronwen turned and began walking back along the beach toward Rossall Hall. She felt better for her run, and somehow her father's plan did not seem so far-fetched anymore. Distant lights twinkled through the fog that was rolling in from the west, and she suddenly realized what a long way she had come.

"My lady," the man's voice called out behind her.

Bronwen kept walking, unwilling to face again the one who had seen her in her humiliation. She didn't care what he reported to his master.

"My lady, you have quite a walk ahead of you." The traveler strode forward to join her. "I shall accompany you to your destination."

"You leave me no choice, I see."

"I am not one to compromise myself, dear lady. I follow the path God has set before me and none other."

"And just who are you?"

"I am called Jacques."

"French. A Norman, as I had suspected."

The man chuckled. "Not nearly as Norman as you are Briton."

As they approached the fortress, Bronwen could see that the guests had not yet begun to disperse. Perhaps no one had missed her, and she could slip quietly into bed beside Gildan.

She turned to go, but he took her arm and studied her face in the moonlight. Then, gently, he drew her into the folds of his hooded cloak. "Perhaps the bride would like the memory of a younger man's embrace to warm her," he whispered.

Astonished, Bronwen attempted to remove his arms from around her waist. But she could not escape his lips as they found her own. The kiss was soft and warm, melting away her resistance like the sun upon the snow. Before she had time to react, he was striding back down the beach.

Bronwen stood stunned for a moment, clutching his woolen mantle about her. Suddenly she cried out, "Wait, Jacques! Your mantle!"

The dark one turned to her. "Keep it for now," he shouted into the wind. "I shall ask for it when we meet again."

* * * * *

Don't miss this deeply moving story,
THE BRITON,
available February 2008
from the new Love Inspired Historical line.

And also look for
HOMESPUN BRIDE
by Jillian Hart,
where a Montana woman discovers that love
is the greatest blessing of all.

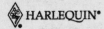

HARLEQUIN®

EVERLASTING LOVE™

Every great love has a story to tell™

The Valentine Gift

featuring
three deeply emotional stories of love that stands the test of time, just in time for Valentine's Day!

USA TODAY bestselling author
Tara Taylor Quinn

Linda Cardillo
and
Jean Brashear

**Available just in time for Valentine's Day
February wherever you buy books.**

www.eHarlequin.com

HEL65427

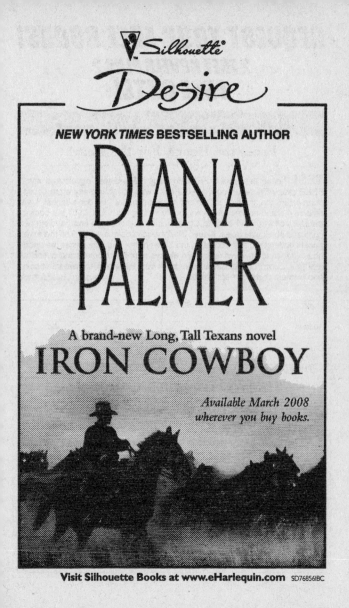

Silhouette®

Desire

NEW YORK TIMES BESTSELLING AUTHOR

DIANA PALMER

A brand-new Long, Tall Texans novel

IRON COWBOY

*Available March 2008
wherever you buy books.*

Visit Silhouette Books at www.eHarlequin.com SD76856IBC

REQUEST YOUR FREE BOOKS!
2 FREE NOVELS PLUS 2
FREE GIFTS!

HARLEQUIN ROMANCE®

From the Heart, For the Heart

YES! Please send me 2 FREE Harlequin Romance® novels and my 2 FREE gifts. After receiving them, if I don't wish to receive any more books, I can return the shipping statement marked "cancel." If I don't cancel, I will receive 4 brand-new novels every month and be billed just $3.57 per book in the U.S., or $4.05 per book in Canada, plus 25¢ shipping and handling per book and applicable taxes, if any*. That's a savings of over 15% off the cover price! I understand that accepting the 2 free books and gifts places me under no obligation to buy anything. I can always return a shipment and cancel at any time. Even if I never buy another book from Harlequin, the two free books and gifts are mine to keep forever.   114 HDN EEV7 314 HDN EEWK

Name	(PLEASE PRINT)	
Address		Apt.
City	State/Prov.	Zip/Postal Code

Signature (if under 18, a parent or guardian must sign)

Mail to the **Harlequin Reader Service®**:
IN U.S.A.: P.O. Box 1867, Buffalo, NY 14240-1867
IN CANADA: P.O. Box 609, Fort Erie, Ontario L2A 5X3

Not valid to current Harlequin Romance subscribers.

Want to try two free books from another line?
Call 1-800-873-8635 or visit www.morefreebooks.com.

* Terms and prices subject to change without notice. NY residents add applicable sales tax. Canadian residents will be charged applicable provincial taxes and GST. This offer is limited to one order per household. All orders subject to approval. Credit or debit balances in a customer's account(s) may be offset by any other outstanding balance owed by or to the customer. Please allow 4 to 6 weeks for delivery.

Your Privacy: Harlequin is committed to protecting your privacy. Our Privacy Policy is available online at www.eHarlequin.com or upon request from the Reader Service. From time to time we make our lists of customers available to reputable firms who may have a product or service of interest to you. If you would prefer we not share your name and address, please check here. ☐

Inside ROMANCE

Stay up-to-date on all your romance reading news!

Inside Romance is a FREE quarterly newsletter highlighting our upcoming series releases and promotions.

Visit

www.eHarlequin.com/InsideRomance

to sign up to receive our complimentary newsletter today!

IRNI I 07

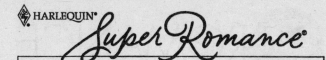

Texas Hold 'Em

When it comes to love, the stakes are high

Sixteen years ago, Luke Chisum dated
Becky Parker on a dare…before going
on to break her heart. Now the former
River Bluff daredevil is back, rekindling
desire and tempting Becky to pick up
where they left off. But this time she has
to resist or Luke could discover the secret
she's kept locked away all these years….

Look for

TEXAS BLUFF

by *Linda Warren*

#1470

Available February 2008
wherever you buy books.

The second book in the deliciously passionate
Heart trilogy by *New York Times* bestselling author

KAT MARTIN

As a viscount's daughter, vivacious Coralee Whitmore
is perfectly placed to write about London's elite in the
outspoken ladies' gazette *Heart to Heart*. But beneath her
fashionable exterior beats the heart of a serious journalist.

So when her sister's death is dismissed as suicide, Corrie vows
to uncover the truth, suspecting that the notorious Earl of
Tremaine was Laurel's lover and the father of her illegitimate
child. But Corrie finds the earl is not all he seems…nor is
she immune to his charms, however much she despises his
caddish ways.

"The first of [a] new series,
Heart of Honor is a grand
way for the author to begin…
Kat Martin has penned
another memorable tale."
—*Historical Romance Writers*

*Heart of
Fire*

*Available the first week of January 2008
wherever paperbacks are sold!*

HARLEQUIN *Romance.*

Coming Next Month

**Ranchers, lords, sheikhs and playboys—the perfect men
to make you sigh this Valentine's Day, from Harlequin Romance®...**

#4003 CATTLE RANCHER, SECRET SON Margaret Way

Have you ever fallen in love at first sight? Gina did—but she knew she could never be good enough for Cal's society family. Now Cal's determined to marry her—but is it to avoid a scandal and claim his son, or because he really loves her?

#4004 RESCUED BY THE SHEIKH Barbara McMahon
Desert Brides

Be swept away to the swirling sands and cool oases of the Moquansaid desert. Lost and alone, Lisa is relieved to be rescued by a handsome stranger. But this sheikh is no ordinary man, and Lisa suddenly begins to feel out of her depth again....

#4005 THE PLAYBOY'S PLAIN JANE Cara Colter

You know the type: confident, sexy, gorgeous—and he knows it. Entrepreneur Dylan simply has *it*. But Katie's no pushover and is determined to steer clear—that is until she starts to see a side of him she never knew existed.

#4006 HER ONE AND ONLY VALENTINE Trish Wylie

Do you find yourself hoping for a special surprise on Valentine's Day? Single mom Rhiannon's about to get a big one! When Kane left, breaking Rhiannon's heart, he didn't know he'd left behind something infinitely precious. But now he's back in town....

#4007 ENGLISH LORD, ORDINARY LADY Fiona Harper
By Royal Appointment

It's so important to be loved for who you *really* are inside. Josie agrees, and thinks new boss Will doesn't look beneath the surface enough. But appearances can be deceptive, especially when moonlit kisses in the castle orchard get in the way!

#4008 EXECUTIVE MOTHER-TO-BE Nicola Marsh
Baby on Board

Career-girl Kristen's spontaneous decision to share one special night with sexy entrepreneur Nathan was crazy—and totally out of character! But now there are two shocks in store—one unexpected baby and one sexy but very familiar new boss....

HRCNM0108